Whispers of the Fallen Tr es

A Battle for Elaria *Spirits*

Copyright © 2024 by Elara Quinn

All rights reserved. No part of this book may be used or reproduced in any form whatsoever without written permission except in the case of brief quotations in critical articles or reviews.

First Edition: October 2024

Table of Contents

Chapter 1 A Whisper in the Woods 1

Chapter 2 Ironhold's Ambition 14

Chapter 3 Secrets of the Ancient Pact 28

Chapter 4 Schemes and Shadows 42

Chapter 5 The Fae's Refusal 56

Chapter 6 Gathering the Lost 76

Chapter 7 Paths Unseen 91

Chapter 8 A Warning Ignored 107

Chapter 9 Desperation and Resolve 123

Chapter 10 Breaking Point 138

Chapter 11 The Forest's Awakening 154

Chapter 12 Limits and Choices 170

Chapter 13 Lines in the Sand 186

Chapter 14 Rallying the Spirits 201

Chapter 15 The Breath of Elaria 217

Epilogue A New Dawn 231

Chapter 1
A Whisper in the Woods

The forest of Elaria was never silent, but today the whispers felt different—agitated, restless. Lira moved through the ancient paths with practiced ease, her feet almost instinctively avoiding roots and fallen branches. The leaves, usually swaying lazily in the midday breeze, seemed to shiver as she passed. It was as if the forest itself were trying to speak to her, louder and more insistent than usual.

Pausing, she pressed her hand against the gnarled bark of a massive oak tree. She closed her eyes, feeling the rough texture under her fingers as she exhaled slowly, her breath syncing with the low hum she could hear reverberating deep within the tree. The sensation wasn't new—she had been communing with the trees since she was a child—but today, the vibrations were almost palpable, the hum turning into something akin to an urgent murmur.

"Calm yourself," she whispered, though it felt as if she were saying it more for her benefit than for the ancient oak. The whispers didn't calm. Instead, they grew sharper, more distinct, until they coalesced into words that sent a chill through her veins.

"Danger approaches…"

Lira's fingers tightened around the bark as if anchoring herself against the weight of the warning. She opened her eyes, the vibrant green of her irises shimmering with a faint glow, a sign of her connection to the Breath of Elaria—the ancient magic that flowed through every living thing in the forest. The trees had warned her before of small disturbances, hunters venturing too deep, or stray spirits unsettled by passing storms, but this was different. It felt darker, and the shadows seemed to deepen as the whispers echoed within her mind.

"What do you mean?" she murmured, her voice barely audible. She leaned closer, her forehead nearly touching the rough bark. The oak's deep groans reverberated through her fingertips.

"A darkness… stirring… at the edge of the world…"

Lira's eyes widened as she tried to focus, grasping at the fleeting glimpses the trees offered her. She saw flashes of darkened skies and the glint of iron, heard distant, pained cries tangled within the relentless clanking of machines. She drew a shuddering breath, stepping back from the oak, its rough surface lingering on her skin like an imprint.

The oak's voice faded, its whispers slipping back into its roots, but the warning lingered in Lira's mind. She turned and made her way through the overgrown paths that wound deeper into the heart of the forest. It wasn't long before she reached a clearing where Elder Ashen stood, his massive branches arching like an ancient, watchful guardian over the grove.

"Elder Ashen," Lira called softly, her voice barely louder than the breeze.

The ancient tree spirit stirred, his low voice groaning through the canopy. "Child," he greeted, his tone creaking with age and a weariness that seemed to seep from his very roots. "You feel it too, don't you?"

Lira nodded, stepping closer. "The whispers are urgent, warning of something… wrong. What is it?" Her voice held an edge of unease that she rarely showed in Elder Ashen's presence.

The great tree was silent for a long moment, his leaves rustling like the sigh of a slumbering giant awakening to a grim reality. When he finally spoke, there was a weight to his words that settled deep in Lira's chest. "Ironhold," he rumbled, the name echoing like a curse. "The old enemy, long separated from us by their ambition, has returned."

"Ironhold?" Lira echoed, confusion knitting her brow. "But they haven't crossed the borders in years. The spirits—"

"The spirits sense their corruption growing," Elder Ashen interrupted, his voice heavy with sadness. "The balance is shifting. Ironhold's hunger for power grows unchecked, and their twisted alchemy reaches for what it does not understand. They seek the breath of Elaria, and their machines…"

Lira clenched her fists, the anger flaring up unbidden. "They seek to take from us again," she said, bitterness slipping into her words. "They would drain the forest's life, enslave its spirits…"

"It is an old tale," Elder Ashen murmured. "One that we have heard before. But it is not history that repeats—it is ambition that remains unlearned."

Lira took a breath, calming herself. "What should I do, Elder?"

The tree spirit's branches creaked as he considered her question. "Be vigilant, child. Listen closely to the whispers, for they will guide you. And remember, this forest thrives on its balance, but it is fragile. We must not act in haste."

Lira nodded, feeling the weight of his words settle on her shoulders. "I will."

As she turned to leave, Elder Ashen's voice called after her. "Lira."

She paused, glancing back over her shoulder.

"There are secrets in these woods that have been lost to time," the ancient spirit said, his voice laced with something akin to regret. "If Ironhold seeks to claim them, it may lead to a fate worse than what came before."

A chill ran through Lira, but she forced herself to nod, steeling her resolve. She could feel the forest watching her, every leaf, every root, as if holding its breath in anticipation. Whatever darkness was brewing, she would be ready.

Leaving the grove, Lira walked with a newfound determination, the soft whispers of the trees no longer mere murmurs but an urgent call to arms.

Lira stood before Elder Ashen, the ancient tree towering over her like a sentinel of times long past. His massive trunk bore deep carvings and knots that marked the passing of countless seasons, the lines etched into his bark resembling faded runes from forgotten eras. Leaves fluttered gently in the breeze, brushing against Lira's face as if offering a silent comfort. She breathed in the scent of earth and moss, a smell that felt like home—familiar, grounding, and eternal.

"Tell me about Ironhold," Lira prompted, her voice barely above a whisper. She rarely asked the ancient tree spirit for details, knowing his memory spanned more lifetimes than any human could comprehend. But something about today—about the urgency of the whispers—made her press for answers.

Elder Ashen's branches rustled, his deep voice resonating through the clearing like a distant thunder. "Ironhold," he began, the name rolling out slowly, like a boulder tumbling from a mountainside, "was once a place of unity, a city that thrived on the old harmony between our world and theirs."

Lira tilted her head, a frown creasing her brow. "Harmony?" she echoed, the word sounding foreign when paired with the image of dark, smoke-filled skies and twisted machines she had glimpsed in her visions.

"Yes," Elder Ashen continued, his voice crackling like dry wood. "There was a time, child, long before the scars of distrust, when humans and spirits walked the same paths. Ironhold's early settlers sought to build—not with the forest's bones, but alongside its breath." His leaves quivered, and a low groan escaped his trunk, almost like a sigh. "But ambition is a disease that feeds on patience, and power is a hunger never easily sated."

Lira shifted her weight, feeling the weight of his words settle heavily on her shoulders. She didn't fully understand the history Elder Ashen spoke of, the time of the Sacred Pact and the Great Harmony. To her, these were tales as old as the roots beneath her feet—whispers of a past that had crumbled long before her birth.

"What happened?" she asked softly.

The old tree spirit remained silent for a moment, as if gathering strength to speak of old wounds. "Ironhold's leaders, in their yearning to tame the wild and harness its magic, broke the Sacred Pact. They captured spirits, twisted their essence, and used their pain to fuel machines of iron and stone." His voice deepened, rough and mournful. "The bond between us was shattered, and the city turned its back on the forest, sealing its gates and turning its eyes inward."

Lira took a step closer, reaching out to touch a knot in Elder Ashen's trunk, her fingers brushing the ridges worn smooth by time. "And now...?" she ventured, her voice tinged with dread.

"They return, but not as they were," Elder Ashen replied, his voice lowering to a near whisper. "Their alchemists have found ways to corrupt the Breath of Elaria, to bend our magic to their will. I feel it in the soil, in the winds, in the cries of the spirits who suffer within their machines."

Lira's fingers curled into a fist against the bark. "We have to stop them," she said, her voice firm despite the unease tightening her chest.

"It is not so simple," Elder Ashen warned, his tone laden with centuries of sorrow. "The balance of Elaria is delicate. We are connected to the Breath, but so too are they. We cannot fight blindly, or we risk becoming like those who wronged us." His branches creaked, and Lira imagined the weight of his words was like an invisible chain, binding her to the responsibility she bore as the forest's protector.

"Then what do we do?" Lira pressed, her frustration slipping into her voice. "Do we just watch as they take more from us?"

Elder Ashen's leaves rustled, a gentle chiding in the breeze. "Patience, child," he urged. "You must listen—not just to the whispers, but to the intentions behind them. The forest remembers its pain, but it also remembers its hope. Not all within Ironhold are lost to ambition."

Lira looked up, meeting the tree spirit's gaze, though his eyes were unseen. She felt the gentle pressure of his words urging caution. "You speak of hope," she said softly, almost accusingly. "But what hope can there be with enemies who enslave our kin?"

"The hope lies not in seeing the enemy as irredeemable," Elder Ashen replied, his voice carrying a deep weariness, "but in seeking those among them who still hear the call of the ancient ways."

For a moment, Lira considered the old spirit's words, turning them over in her mind. Her memories of the vision—of iron machines and twisted spirits—were raw, their pain echoing in her thoughts. But Elder Ashen's voice held a conviction that was hard to ignore, a reminder that not all conflicts had clear sides.

"Elder, if there are those in Ironhold who remember, how will I find them?" she asked, her tone softer, almost pleading.

"By listening," he answered. "The whispers will guide you to where the paths of fate intertwine."

The ancient tree's words lingered in the air like leaves drifting slowly to the forest floor. Lira closed her eyes, trying to steady the storm of emotions within her. Elder Ashen's wisdom was a constant in her life, a reminder of the forest's endurance through the ages. But his words also carried a warning—a reminder that rushing to act could lead to devastation.

"Thank you," she murmured, though her heart still felt heavy with doubt.

"Remember, Lira," Elder Ashen's voice whispered as she turned to leave, "Ironhold's machines may be loud, but it is the silence between their clamor that holds the truth."

As Lira made her way back through the winding paths of Elaria, she couldn't shake the feeling that the balance Elder Ashen spoke of was far more fragile than she had ever imagined. Each step took her deeper into the heart of the forest, and yet, in her mind, she felt the pull of Ironhold's shadow looming at its edges.

Fenn adjusted the lens of his brass eyeglasses, the dim lantern on his desk casting flickering light over the blueprint sprawled before him. He tapped his pencil thoughtfully on the edge of the paper, his brow furrowed in concentration. The schematic was intricate, almost beautiful in its complexity—each line, each mechanical joint, a testament to the ingenuity of Ironhold's engineering. But something gnawed at him, a feeling he couldn't quite put into words.

"You're staring at that thing like it's gonna sprout legs and dance," came a voice from behind. Fenn looked up to see Brayden leaning against the doorway, arms crossed and a smirk playing on his lips.

"Maybe it will," Fenn replied, offering a half-hearted grin. He leaned back in his chair, stretching his shoulders as he set down his pencil. "Wouldn't surprise me with these new models."

Brayden chuckled, stepping into the room and glancing at the blueprint. "The Chancellor's really pushing these Corrupted Spirit Engines, huh? And here you are, still poking at them like a curious squirrel."

Fenn's smile faded slightly. "It's just… something about the power source doesn't sit right with me. We've always used energy from the spirit engines, but these…" He tapped the corner of the blueprint where the core of the engine was sketched. "These feel different."

"What do you mean?" Brayden asked, taking a seat on the edge of Fenn's desk.

Fenn hesitated, as if searching for the right words. "The old spirit engines—they were imperfect, but the energy flow made sense. The spirits used were… well, less volatile. But these new engines," he said, pointing at the diagram of the main containment chamber, "require a constant infusion of something more potent, more… alive."

Brayden raised an eyebrow, the smirk slipping into a frown. "You're not going soft on us, are you?" he teased, but there was an edge to his voice. "The Chancellor says these engines are the future. They'll power Ironhold's growth, keep the factories running, and secure our place in history. He's putting his faith in you to refine the designs."

"I know, I know," Fenn replied quickly. "I just can't stop thinking about how the containment runes have to be reinforced daily, or how the spirits… I mean, the essence inside them keeps resisting." He leaned back, rubbing the back of his neck as if trying to ease a tension that had settled there. "Why would the energy resist if it were truly harnessed properly?"

"Fenn," Brayden's voice was firm, his eyes narrowing slightly. "It's not our job to ask why the Chancellor's engines work the way they do. It's our job to make them work better."

Fenn sighed, letting out a quiet chuckle to ease the tension. "Maybe you're right," he said, but his voice lacked conviction. "Still, don't you ever wonder… if there's a reason for that resistance?"

Brayden shook his head with a chuckle. "You always were the thinker, Fenn," he said, standing and giving his friend a reassuring pat on the shoulder. "But sometimes, thinking gets in the way of progress. Trust in the Chancellor's vision. He's leading Ironhold to greatness."

"Greatness," Fenn echoed softly, his eyes drifting back to the blueprint. The lines seemed to blur under his gaze, the design shifting into something almost sinister. He blinked and shook his head, trying to clear the unsettling thoughts that lingered at the edges of his mind. "Yeah, greatness."

Brayden turned to leave but paused at the doorway. "Look," he said, his voice taking on a more serious tone, "I know you've got your doubts, but just remember what we're working towards. A future where Ironhold isn't dependent on those old, unreliable engines. A future where we're free from the limitations of the past."

Fenn nodded absently, not trusting himself to speak. He watched Brayden leave, the door swinging shut behind him with a soft click that echoed in the quiet room. Once he was alone, Fenn let out a long breath, the weight of his thoughts pressing down on his chest.

"Why does something so innovative feel so wrong?" he muttered to himself, tracing the lines of the blueprint with his fingertips.

"Talking to yourself again?" came another voice from the corner, this time softer and laced with a touch of amusement. Fenn glanced up to see Mara, another engineer and one of the few people who understood his unease. She leaned against the wall, her arms crossed, eyes watching him with quiet curiosity.

"Maybe I am," Fenn replied with a small, tired smile. "Keeps me from going mad with all these calculations."

"Or maybe you're already mad," Mara shot back, her eyes narrowing in mock suspicion. But her tone shifted, more serious now. "You really don't like these new engines, do you?"

Fenn hesitated. He had never voiced his concerns openly, not even to Mara, but the growing knot in his chest begged for release. "It's not just the design," he admitted, his voice barely above a whisper. "It's the energy inside them. It's not just fuel—it feels… alive, and angry."

Mara was silent, her gaze searching his face for a long moment. "Fenn, if you really believe something's off, you need to tread carefully. Questioning the Chancellor's orders isn't exactly safe."

"I know," Fenn replied, the weight of his uncertainty pressing down harder with each word. "But if there's even a chance that what we're doing is wrong…"

Mara stepped forward, her hand resting on his shoulder. "Just… be careful, alright? Whatever you decide to do, you need to stay safe."

Fenn offered a small, grateful nod. "Thanks, Mara."

She smiled faintly, giving his shoulder a squeeze before stepping back. "And maybe get some sleep. You look like you've been fighting a battle in your head all night."

"Maybe I have," Fenn replied, half-joking. But as she left, the lingering unease in his chest remained, a quiet whisper of doubt that refused to be silenced.

Alone once more, Fenn stared at the blueprint, the lines shifting like restless shadows. He tried to push the doubts away, but the question continued to echo in his mind, as relentless and insistent as a distant, unyielding hum.

"What have we unleashed?"

Chapter 2
Ironhold's Ambition

The winds along the edge of Elaria carried the scent of iron and smoke, mingling uneasily with the fresh scent of moss and pine. Lira stood at the forest's border, her senses alert to the slightest shift in the earth. She didn't need to see the encroaching machines to know they were there—she could feel them. Every clank of iron, every rumble of the ground, reverberated through her bones like the echoes of a distant storm.

"It's begun," she whispered, her voice a mere breath on the wind. She placed her hand against a young birch tree, its bark smooth and trembling under her fingers.

"Pain... Help us..." The voices of the spirits within the trees were faint, almost drowned out by the steady hum of the approaching machines. Lira clenched her teeth, forcing herself to breathe slowly. She could feel the life draining from the birch, the magic fading as roots were severed deep beneath the soil.

"Stay strong," she murmured, trying to push comfort into her voice despite the dread clawing at her chest.

The ground quivered beneath her feet, and in the distance, the first tree fell with a heavy, soul-wrenching crash. It was not just a sound—it was a cry, an anguished wail that tore through the silence of the forest. Lira's eyes closed tightly, the weight of the spirit's pain pressing against her mind.

"No," she whispered, the word slipping out like a plea. Her fingers dug into the birch's bark as if trying to anchor herself against the tide of emotions flooding her senses.

From the shadows, a dry voice cut through her thoughts. "You can't save them all."

Lira turned to see a spirit creature perched on a nearby stone, its shape indistinct but familiar. The creature was part wolf, part mist—a guardian of the forest, bound to protect its secrets. Its eyes, bright and piercing, watched her with a mixture of pity and warning.

"Farael," Lira breathed, recognizing the spirit. "They're—"

"Dying?" Farael finished, his voice echoing like the rustle of dead leaves. "Yes. They are." His gaze shifted toward the source of the disturbance, a dark line where the towering trees of Elaria met the desolation wrought by Ironhold's machines. "You feel them, don't you? The roots, the spirits… all breaking."

Lira nodded, unable to speak. The pain of the forest flowed through her, every tremor and crack like an open wound. "They've crossed the border," she finally managed, her voice tight with anger.

"Borders mean nothing to men with iron and ambition," Farael said, his voice tinged with ancient bitterness. "You should know this by now, Guardian."

Lira's hands tightened into fists. "We have to stop them."

The spirit's form shifted, mist swirling around its legs as it moved closer. "And how would you do that?" Farael asked. "Their machines are relentless, their intent unwavering. You can't fight iron with whispers, Lira."

"Then I'll do more than whisper," Lira replied, her eyes narrowing. "I can feel them—spirits trapped inside those machines. If I can reach them—"

"You'll reach nothing but death," Farael interrupted sharply. "You're not ready."

Lira's temper flared, and the air around her seemed to thrum with barely restrained power. "Then tell me what I *should* do!" she demanded, her voice rising. "Stand here and watch as they destroy everything? Let them tear apart our home, kill the spirits?"

Farael's eyes softened, and for a moment, the ancient sorrow in them was almost unbearable to face. "Sometimes, standing and watching is all we can do," he said quietly. "Until we are ready to act."

"I can't accept that," Lira replied, her voice trembling with frustration. "There has to be a way to fight back. There has to be…"

"There is," Farael said, his voice a low murmur. "But not now. Not like this." He lifted his gaze, looking out beyond the treeline where the distant shapes of the machines moved slowly, methodically, like a creeping illness. "Ironhold is not just machines and men. It is a storm that has been brewing for years, and it will not be calmed by a single drop of rain."

Lira turned her eyes to the distant shapes, her fists unclenching slightly. "But if I do nothing—"

"You are not doing nothing," Farael corrected. "You are *listening*. And that is the first step to understanding."

The ground beneath them shook again, a deeper rumble this time, followed by another crash. Lira flinched, her breath catching as she felt another spirit's life slip away. "I can't just listen while they suffer," she whispered.

Farael was silent for a long moment, his form blurring at the edges like mist caught in a restless breeze. When he finally spoke, his voice was a soft whisper, almost like the wind passing through dead leaves. "Then promise me one thing, Guardian of Elaria," he said, his eyes locking with hers. "When the time comes to act, do not let your rage blind you to what must be saved."

Lira met his gaze, her own eyes burning with unshed tears. "I promise," she said quietly, the weight of the vow settling heavily in her chest.

The spirit's form shimmered and faded into the shadows, leaving Lira alone with the encroaching darkness. She turned her eyes back to the distant line of iron and smoke, her resolve hardening like the roots beneath her feet. Every tree that fell, every spirit that cried out—it all drove the urgency deeper into her heart.

"I'm listening," she whispered, and the wind carried her words through the forest, a soft murmur of defiance amidst the roar of machines.

Lira darted through the trees, the air thick with the scent of iron and oil. Her breath came in sharp, ragged bursts as she raced toward the sounds of groaning timber and grinding gears. The forest seemed to recoil with each footfall, the vibrations running through her body like faint echoes of pain. Spirits within the ancient trunks whispered warnings, urging caution, but she pushed on, driven by an urgency she couldn't ignore.

She broke through the last line of trees and skidded to a halt. Before her, the clearing was a battlefield of iron against nature. Great hulking machines, with wheels groaning under their weight, loomed like monsters, their dark metal bodies reflecting the dim light. Massive saw-blades spun, their teeth biting into the flesh of ancient oaks, and Lira's heart clenched at every shuddering scream that reverberated through the earth.

Lira raised a trembling hand, reaching toward a towering iron machine that had locked its claws around a tree's roots. She murmured a prayer, and a soft, green light flickered between her fingers as she called on the Breath of Elaria. The roots beneath the machine began to move, twisting and tangling in response to her will, like serpents awakening from slumber.

"Release it," she commanded, her voice steady despite the turmoil inside her.

For a moment, the machine's wheels stuttered, its iron claws trembling as if fighting against an unseen force. Lira's hope flared, but then she felt the pushback—an overwhelming surge of foreign energy that lashed out like a beast, snapping the roots with ease. Her connection with the forest wavered, the green light in her hand flickering and then dying out.

"Damn it," Lira hissed, her breath escaping in a frustrated rush.

"Who are you?" a voice called out sharply from behind one of the machines.

Lira spun, her eyes narrowing at the sight of a small group of engineers emerging from behind the iron contraption. They wore thick, soot-stained uniforms, their faces masked by heavy goggles. But one figure stood out—a young man with bright, intelligent eyes that watched her with something other than the cold indifference she had come to expect from Ironhold.

The man pushed up his goggles, revealing a face marked with curiosity more than malice. He looked at her not with fear or disdain, but with awe.

"Who is she?" one of the other engineers muttered, keeping a hand on his weapon.

"Lira," she replied, her voice firm. "And you're killing the forest."

The man with the bright eyes took a cautious step forward. "Lira," he repeated, the name rolling off his tongue like an unfamiliar word. "Are you… one of the forest spirits?"

"No," Lira snapped, her anger boiling over. "But I speak for them."

The man hesitated, and for a moment, Lira saw a flicker of something—doubt, maybe even understanding—in his gaze. But then one of the older engineers barked an order, and the moment passed. The group readied their tools, and the machines rumbled to life once more.

"Stop!" Lira shouted, her voice laced with desperation. She thrust out her hands, drawing on every ounce of the forest's magic she could muster. The roots surged once more, rising like waves of earth and wood, wrapping around the machines' legs.

The man, Fenn, watched in stunned silence as the ground seemed to come alive beneath his feet. "By the stars…" he whispered, awe creeping into his voice. But the other engineers weren't so easily swayed. They shouted commands and tightened their grips on their weapons.

"Disengage! Disengage now!" one of them yelled, and the machines' iron claws snapped free of the roots with a violent jerk.

Lira felt the recoil like a punch to her gut, her connection severing with a painful snap. She staggered, nearly falling to her knees as the machines continued their relentless advance. She tried to call the roots again, but the green light in her hands sputtered and failed. She was pushing too hard, too fast—her magic was slipping from her grasp, like water through her fingers.

"Please," she said, her voice a broken whisper. "You don't understand what you're doing."

Fenn stepped forward, ignoring the shouts of his colleagues. "Wait!" he called, holding up a hand. "Listen to her!"

"What are you doing, Fenn?" one of the older engineers demanded, his voice gruff with authority. "She's disrupting the operation!"

Fenn shook his head, his eyes never leaving Lira. "She's… not like the others," he muttered, more to himself than anyone else. "She's connected… somehow."

The older engineer spat on the ground. "She's a witch, that's what she is! And if she's in league with the spirits, then she's our enemy."

Lira's eyes met Fenn's, and in that brief moment, she saw the confusion and conflict warring within him. He didn't look at her like the others did—he wasn't blinded by hatred or fear. He was curious, searching for answers in a world that offered only rigid lines and dark shadows.

But there was no time to find common ground. The engineers resumed their commands, and the machines advanced once more. Lira felt the ground tremble beneath her, the spirits' cries growing fainter, more distant. She couldn't hold back the tears that burned in her eyes as another ancient tree shuddered and fell with a deafening crash.

"Go!" Farael's voice rang out, urgent and sharp, somewhere in the back of her mind. "Leave now, or you'll die with them!"

Lira's heart wrenched, but she knew Farael was right. Her magic was nearly depleted, and she couldn't face the machines alone. She cast one last desperate look at Fenn, silently pleading for him to understand, to do something—anything—to stop this madness.

But Fenn was frozen in place, torn between duty and doubt.

Lira turned and fled, her feet pounding against the earth as the forest wept around her. The sounds of the machines faded into the distance, replaced by the whisper of the wind and the faint, lingering echoes of spirits lost to iron and ambition.

Fenn walked through the twisting corridors of Ironhold's Alchemical Towers, the faint, acrid smell of burnt metal and sulfur lingering in the air. The voices of the other engineers faded into a dull hum as he made his way deeper into the complex. His thoughts were a restless storm, swirling around a single, indelible image: the girl in the forest, her hands glowing with green light, speaking to the trees as if they could hear her.

"She's connected… somehow," he murmured under his breath, echoing his words from the clearing. He stopped outside a heavy door marked with intricate runes, the entrance to Chancellor Corvin's study. A chill ran through him, and for a moment, he considered turning back, but he forced himself to knock.

"Enter," came a smooth, commanding voice from within.

Fenn took a steadying breath and opened the door. Chancellor Aleron Corvin stood at a large window overlooking the city's sprawling factories, his back turned to the entrance. The Chancellor's silhouette was sharp and imposing, framed by the dark stone walls and the faint red light that filtered in through the smog-choked sky. He wore his usual dark, rune-etched robes, his silver hair tied back with precise neatness.

"Fenn," Corvin said without turning, his voice carrying a note of mild surprise. "I wasn't expecting you."

"I—I wanted to report on today's progress, sir," Fenn replied, trying to keep his voice steady.

Corvin turned slowly, his steel-blue eyes locking onto Fenn's with unnerving intensity. "I trust all is proceeding as planned?"

"Yes, sir," Fenn began, choosing his words carefully. "We encountered minimal resistance at the forest's edge. The machines performed well, and the extraction of resources has begun."

The Chancellor studied Fenn in silence for a moment, as if searching for a hidden meaning in his words. "And?" he prompted.

Fenn swallowed, feeling the weight of Corvin's gaze. "And… the containment runes held, sir. There were no major disruptions."

A lie, or at least a partial one. He could still hear the sound of roots breaking, the cries of the spirits caught within the machines. But he had rehearsed this report in his mind, and the lie came out almost effortlessly.

Corvin nodded, a satisfied smile tugging at the corner of his mouth. "Good. The stability of the new spirit engines is paramount. We cannot afford any setbacks in our progress."

"Of course, sir," Fenn agreed quickly, trying to focus on the words rather than the thoughts roiling beneath them. But even as he spoke, he couldn't shake the memory of the girl—Lira. He hadn't told Corvin about her, and he didn't intend to. He wasn't sure why; it felt like a fragile secret, something he needed to understand before it was exposed to scrutiny.

The Chancellor's eyes narrowed slightly, as if sensing the hesitation in Fenn's voice. "Is there something else on your mind?" he asked, his voice deceptively soft.

Fenn forced himself to meet the Chancellor's gaze. "No, sir. Just… the usual adjustments to the designs, but nothing of immediate concern."

Corvin's smile widened, but the chill in his eyes remained. "You are a diligent engineer, Fenn. One of my finest. Do not let doubts cloud your purpose. Ironhold's future depends on our ability to harness the power within Elaria—nothing must stand in our way."

"Understood, sir," Fenn replied, nodding quickly. But inside, his thoughts were far from certain.

As he left the Chancellor's study, his mind was still racing. He replayed the encounter with Lira in the clearing, trying to make sense of what he had seen. The way she had spoken to the trees, the roots responding to her call—it was like nothing he had ever witnessed. He had always believed that the spirits Ironhold captured were merely sources of raw power, remnants of ancient magic that no longer served a purpose. But now…

"Are they really alive?" he whispered, almost afraid of the answer.

He descended the winding staircase, his footsteps echoing against the stone walls. When he reached the lower level, he found Mara waiting for him near one of the iron-forged doors that led to the machinery workshops. She was leaning against the wall, arms crossed, her expression unreadable.

"Chancellor didn't keep you long," she remarked, her voice casual but her eyes sharp.

"Just a routine report," Fenn replied, trying to sound nonchalant.

"Routine," Mara repeated, raising an eyebrow. "You looked like you'd seen a ghost when you went in."

"Maybe I did," Fenn muttered under his breath, more to himself than to her. He shook his head quickly, forcing a smile. "It's nothing."

"Sure it is," Mara said, not buying it for a second. She studied him for a moment, then sighed. "Look, if something's bothering you, you need to deal with it before it eats you alive."

Fenn hesitated, glancing around to make sure no one else was within earshot. "Mara," he said quietly, "have you ever wondered if… if we're doing the right thing?"

Mara's eyes widened slightly, and she opened her mouth to respond, but then she caught herself and glanced down the corridor. "You can't talk like that here," she whispered sharply. "Not if you value your life."

"I know," Fenn replied, lowering his voice. "But something happened today, in the forest. There was a girl—"

"A girl?" Mara cut him off, her eyes narrowing. "From Elaria?"

Fenn nodded slowly, trying to find the right words. "She—she wasn't just from the forest, Mara. She was… *connected* to it, like she could command it."

"Command it?" Mara repeated, her skepticism plain. "You're not making sense, Fenn."

"I know it sounds crazy," he admitted, running a hand through his hair. "But I saw it with my own eyes. The trees… they moved when she spoke to them."

Mara's expression softened, the skepticism giving way to concern. "Fenn, you've been working too hard. You're probably just seeing things. The pressure's getting to you."

"Maybe," he replied, though he didn't believe it. The memory of Lira's voice, the roots responding to her command, was too vivid to dismiss as a trick of the mind.

Mara placed a hand on his arm, squeezing gently. "Get some rest," she urged. "You're no good to anyone if you drive yourself mad."

Fenn forced a smile and nodded, but as he walked away, the seeds of doubt continued to grow, taking root in the corners of his mind. He couldn't stop questioning, couldn't stop wondering if everything he had been taught about the spirits, about Elaria, was a lie.

And the more he tried to bury the doubts, the more they seemed to whisper to him, like echoes of a voice he couldn't forget.

Chapter 3
Secrets of the Ancient Pact

Lira walked slowly through the ancient paths of Elaria, her feet instinctively avoiding the roots and overgrown patches as if the forest itself were guiding her. But today, something felt wrong. The whispers that usually filled her senses were barely more than a murmur, distant and faint like echoes lost in a storm. It was as if the forest, which had always embraced her like a living, breathing presence, was now holding its breath.

She reached the heart of the grove where Elder Ashen stood—a towering oak whose ancient branches stretched like arms over the clearing. The air around him was heavy, thick with a quiet tension that sent a chill up Lira's spine. She pressed her hand against the rough bark, closing her eyes and trying to ground herself in the familiar texture.

"Elder Ashen," she whispered, almost as if she were afraid to disturb the silence. Her voice trembled, not with fear, but with a desperate need for answers. "Why can't I hear them?"

For a long moment, there was nothing but the rustling of leaves and the faint groan of wood shifting in the breeze. Lira's fingers tightened against the bark, feeling the slow, steady hum beneath her palm. Finally, Elder Ashen's deep voice resonated through her fingers like the low rumble of distant thunder.

"Child of the forest," he greeted, his tone weary, heavy with the weight of centuries. "The whispers have not faded from you alone."

Lira frowned, pressing her forehead against the oak's rough surface. "What does that mean? What's happening?"

Elder Ashen's branches swayed slightly, his voice carrying a note of deep sadness. "The balance of Elaria is slipping, Lira. There is a darkness growing at the edges of our world, reaching for what it does not understand."

"Is it Ironhold?" Lira asked, her voice barely above a whisper. She didn't need confirmation; she could feel the truth in the way the forest seemed to shiver with every passing moment.

"The old enemy," Elder Ashen rumbled, the name Ironhold hanging in the air like a curse. "Their ambition blinds them, and their hunger knows no bounds. They seek to control what was never meant to be tamed."

Lira lifted her head, her vibrant green eyes shimmering with a faint glow. She looked up at the ancient tree, her hands trembling with barely restrained anger. "Then we need to stop them," she said, her voice firm, unyielding. "We can't just let them take what belongs to Elaria."

The ancient oak groaned, his branches creaking as if the weight of her words pressed down upon him. "Rushing into this fight would only lead to ruin, child. The forest thrives on its balance, but that balance is fragile."

Lira clenched her fists, frustration bubbling up within her. "I don't understand! If we don't act now, Ironhold will destroy everything. How can you ask me to wait when the forest is suffering?"

"Patience is not inaction," Elder Ashen replied softly. "It is the wisdom to wait for the right moment, to understand what must be done and what must be avoided."

"Right moment?" Lira echoed, disbelief and anger threading through her voice. "How can there be a 'right moment' when Ironhold is already here, tearing through the forest?"

Elder Ashen was silent for a moment, his leaves rustling in a way that sounded almost like a sigh. "There is an old pact, Lira," he said, his voice deepening with the weight of ancient memories. "A promise made long before your time—a promise that must not be broken."

"A promise?" Lira's voice wavered, confusion and frustration warring within her. "What kind of promise?"

Elder Ashen's branches creaked, the deep groans reverberating through the clearing. "One that was made to protect both the spirits and those who dwell in this land. To break it would be to invite chaos, not just upon Elaria, but upon all who call it home."

Lira shook her head, feeling the sting of tears at the corners of her eyes. "Why won't you tell me what this promise is?" she pleaded, her voice breaking slightly. "If I'm supposed to protect this forest, why are you keeping secrets from me?"

The ancient tree was silent for what felt like an eternity, the only sound the faint rustling of leaves in the wind. Finally, his voice came, heavy and resigned. "Because some truths are burdens that should not be borne alone," he said quietly. "And there are some wounds that time alone cannot heal."

Lira took a step back, her fingers slipping away from the bark. She stared at the great oak, feeling a deep sense of helplessness wash over her. She wanted to argue, to demand more answers, but something in Elder Ashen's voice stopped her—a deep, unspoken pain that echoed through his words.

"Then what am I supposed to do?" she asked, her voice barely more than a whisper.

"Listen," Elder Ashen replied softly. "Listen to the whispers of the forest, even if they are faint. There is wisdom in their silence, and guidance in their stillness."

Lira closed her eyes, taking a slow, shaky breath. She could still feel the whispers, but they were so distant, so elusive. It felt as if the very heart of Elaria was holding its breath, waiting for something she couldn't yet understand.

"I'll listen," she murmured, her voice almost breaking. "But I can't promise that I'll wait forever."

"You are the forest's guardian, Lira," Elder Ashen said, his voice gentle despite the gravity of his words. "And the forest is yours to protect. But remember, even the mightiest trees grow slowly and patiently, their roots seeking out the nourishment they need."

Lira nodded slowly, swallowing back the lingering frustration. "I'll try," she said softly, though her heart still ached with uncertainty.

As she turned to leave the grove, the forest seemed to watch her, every leaf and root holding its breath in anticipation. Whatever darkness was approaching, Lira knew one thing for certain: she couldn't afford to wait for too long. Time was slipping through her fingers, and with each passing moment, the whispers of Elaria grew more urgent.

Fenn leaned over his desk, adjusting the lens of his brass eyeglasses as he peered at the schematic laid out before him. The dim lantern light flickered, casting dancing shadows across the lines and notations of the design. He tapped his pencil lightly on the edge of the paper, brow furrowed in concentration. The new spirit engines were complex, even beautiful in their ingenuity, but something about them gnawed at him—something he couldn't quite define.

"These new cores," Fenn muttered to himself, tracing a finger along the sketched containment chamber. "They're too... reactive."

The containment chamber at the heart of the new spirit engine was unlike the older models. It required a constant infusion of energy—more volatile, more unstable. Fenn had been an engineer long enough to recognize the signs of something pushed beyond its natural limits. He leaned back, rubbing the back of his neck, trying to shake the growing unease that settled over him like a heavy fog.

As he stood there, staring at the schematic, his thoughts wandered back to the Chancellor's last briefing. Chancellor Corvin had been confident—unwavering in his belief that these new engines would secure Ironhold's future. But it wasn't the Chancellor's words that stuck with Fenn; it was the way he spoke of the spirits—dismissive, as if they were merely fuel, no different than coal or oil.

"They're not just energy…" Fenn whispered, his voice trailing off as he flipped through a set of old research notes piled next to his desk. He had read these notes before, written by engineers who had worked on the first spirit engines decades ago. There had been warnings back then, hints of resistance within the energy source, described as almost alive.

Fenn's fingers hovered over the worn pages, his pulse quickening. The notes spoke of containment failures, of energy that seemed to fight back against the runes designed to hold it. There were mentions of incidents where the engines had gone out of control, and references to old runic symbols meant to reinforce the seals. The more he read, the more the pit of dread in his stomach grew.

"Why would the energy resist?" Fenn muttered, flipping through the pages faster now. His unease deepened into something sharper—a fear that the Chancellor wasn't telling them everything. Or perhaps, worse, that the Chancellor didn't understand what he was dealing with.

Lost in thought, Fenn almost didn't hear the knock on his door.

"Fenn?" Brayden's voice came from the other side, impatient and tinged with amusement. "Are you in there, or have you been absorbed by your own thoughts?"

Fenn blinked, tearing his gaze away from the pages. "Come in," he called, trying to steady his voice.

The door creaked open, and Brayden entered, his usual smirk in place. He leaned casually against the doorframe, arms crossed. "You're always in here, staring at those blueprints like they're going to reveal some grand secret," he said with a chuckle.

"Maybe they will," Fenn replied, attempting a half-hearted grin. But the weight of what he had just read pressed on his mind, making it hard to find humor in anything.

"Corvin's got you working double-time on those new cores, huh?" Brayden continued, stepping closer to the desk and peering over Fenn's shoulder. "The Chancellor's really pushing for this next phase. It's like he's got a fire under him."

Fenn swallowed, glancing down at the notes before closing the folder. "Yeah," he murmured, his voice distracted. "Pushing hard."

Brayden studied him for a moment, his eyes narrowing slightly. "You seem off. What's eating at you?"

Fenn hesitated, then shook his head. "Nothing," he lied, feeling the words taste bitter on his tongue. "Just… trying to wrap my head around these new designs."

"Well," Brayden said with a shrug, "don't think too hard. Just trust that the Chancellor knows what he's doing. He's leading us to greatness."

"Greatness," Fenn echoed softly, more to himself than to Brayden. The word felt heavy—hollow, even. Was that what this was? Greatness?

Brayden slapped him on the back, breaking Fenn's train of thought. "You always were the thinker," he said with a grin. "Don't let it get in the way of progress, alright?"

Fenn forced a smile, nodding. "Yeah… progress."

After Brayden left, Fenn let out a slow breath, feeling the tension return. He couldn't shake the feeling that something was being overlooked—something crucial. He turned back to the blueprints, his gaze drawn once more to the core's containment chamber. There were runes etched around the chamber's edge, intricate and unfamiliar. He had never seen these particular symbols before, and they weren't listed in any of the standard references.

Driven by a mix of curiosity and dread, Fenn traced the runes with his finger. They almost seemed to hum beneath his touch, a faint vibration that made his skin tingle. He frowned, leaning closer. The language was unlike anything he had been trained to use, its characters sharp and angular, almost aggressive.

"What are you?" he murmured, flipping back through the design documents. He turned page after page, searching for an explanation, but found none. It was as if the runes had been added as an afterthought—something the engineers weren't meant to question.

His heart beat faster as he examined the containment chamber more closely. There, hidden beneath a reinforced panel, he noticed a small compartment he hadn't seen before. It was subtle—almost intentionally concealed. He pried it open with the edge of his pencil, and inside, he found a set of notes, written in the same angular script.

The hairs on the back of his neck stood up as he stared at the symbols. He didn't understand them, but their presence here, hidden away, spoke volumes. Someone had gone to great lengths to keep this compartment secret. And if there was one thing Fenn had learned in his years as an engineer, it was that secrecy rarely meant good intentions.

"What is Corvin hiding?" Fenn whispered, his voice barely audible.

He closed the hidden compartment, his mind racing. The Chancellor's motivations, the old research warnings, the unfamiliar runes—it all pointed to something darker than mere ambition. For the first time, Fenn felt a deep, gnawing fear that he was part of something far more dangerous than he had realized.

And for the first time, he wasn't sure if he could just follow orders anymore.

Lira moved swiftly through the dense woods, frustration simmering just beneath the surface. The air was thick with the scent of pine and damp earth, but it did little to soothe her nerves. She kept her pace steady, her breaths measured, but her thoughts were racing. The encounter with Elder Ashen earlier had left her feeling restless and uncertain. For every question she asked, he gave answers wrapped in riddles and warnings.

As she approached the heart of the grove, where Elder Ashen stood like an ancient sentinel, Lira forced herself to slow down. Her boots crunched softly over the fallen leaves as she entered the clearing. The great oak's branches were still, almost expectant, as if they had been waiting for her to return.

"Elder Ashen," she called, her voice carrying a note of urgency she didn't bother to hide. "I need to understand. You spoke of an ancient pact—something that prevents you from taking direct action. What is it? And why haven't you told me before?"

The old tree spirit didn't answer right away. His massive branches rustled gently in the breeze, a sound almost like the sigh of a weary old man. When his voice finally came, it was deep and deliberate, each word chosen with care.

"Some knowledge is a burden, Lira," he said softly, the vibration of his voice echoing through the clearing. "And some promises are not easily broken."

"But this isn't about me," Lira pressed, stepping closer and placing her hand against the rough bark. "It's about the forest. It's about protecting the spirits, the Breath of Elaria—everything that Ironhold threatens. Why keep secrets from me when lives are at stake?"

Elder Ashen's branches creaked, his leaves trembling slightly. "The pact was made long ago, in a time when the world was different," he replied. "It was forged to keep the balance between our realm and theirs, to prevent a rift that could tear both worlds apart. To break that pact would risk unleashing forces even I cannot control."

"Then tell me what those forces are," Lira demanded, her voice rising despite herself. "How can I be expected to protect the forest if I don't even know what I'm up against?"

The great oak seemed to shudder slightly, as if under the weight of memories too heavy to bear. "You are a guardian of the forest, Lira," he said, his voice low and almost sorrowful. "But there are truths that even guardians should not seek to uncover lightly. Knowledge is a double-edged blade—sharp and deadly, even to those who wield it."

Lira pulled her hand back from the bark, frustration and confusion churning within her. "You keep telling me to be patient, to wait for the right moment. But Ironhold isn't waiting. They're moving forward, and if we don't act, we'll lose everything."

Elder Ashen's branches swayed gently, his leaves rustling like a soft warning. "Patience is not the absence of action, Lira," he said, a hint of firmness in his tone. "It is the wisdom to act when the time is right. To strike before you are ready is to invite chaos."

"And what if there is no right time?" Lira shot back, her voice edged with desperation. "What if waiting just makes things worse?"

The ancient tree was silent for a moment, as if considering her words. When he spoke again, his voice was tinged with regret. "There is more at stake here than the present struggle," he said quietly. "The Breath of Elaria is not just the lifeblood of the forest—it is the thread that binds all living things. To disturb that balance would have consequences far beyond what you can see."

Lira took a step back, shaking her head. "You're asking me to trust in a promise I don't understand, to wait when the forest is crying out for help," she said, her voice breaking slightly. "How am I supposed to make that choice?"

Elder Ashen's leaves rustled softly, almost like a whisper. "Trust in the forest, child," he murmured. "And trust in yourself. You have the strength to protect what matters, even if you cannot yet see the path clearly."

Lira turned away, feeling the weight of his words settle heavily on her shoulders. She wanted to trust him, to believe that he knew what was best, but every fiber of her being was screaming at her to act, to fight, to do something.

"Is there no other way?" she asked, her voice barely more than a whisper. "No other way to keep the promise and protect the forest?"

For a moment, the clearing was silent, the only sound the faint rustling of leaves in the wind. Elder Ashen's voice, when it came, was almost mournful. "There are always choices, Lira," he said softly. "But not all choices lead to the same end. Some paths, once taken, cannot be undone."

Lira felt a chill run through her, as if the very air around her had grown colder. She closed her eyes, trying to steady her breathing. She needed to think, to clear her mind. But all she could feel was the urgency, the sense of impending danger that seemed to press down on her like a storm cloud.

"I'll try to be patient," she said finally, her voice shaky but determined. "But I can't promise that I'll wait forever."

The ancient oak's branches swayed gently, as if acknowledging her resolve. "You must find your own path, Lira," he replied, his voice carrying a note of quiet acceptance. "And when the time comes, the forest will stand with you."

Lira took a deep breath, nodding slowly. She didn't know if she fully understood what Elder Ashen was trying to tell her, but she knew one thing: she couldn't afford to make a mistake, not when so much was at stake.

As she turned to leave the grove, she felt the weight of his gaze on her back, the silent expectation of a thousand years of wisdom watching her every step. She knew she couldn't wait forever, but for now, she would trust in his words and search for another way.

"Thank you, Elder," she murmured softly, her voice almost lost in the rustle of leaves.

The wind carried her words through the clearing, and as Lira walked away, she couldn't shake the feeling that the forest was holding its breath, waiting for something—waiting for her to find the path that only she could walk.

Chapter 4
Schemes and Shadows

The path to the Fae Court was one Lira had traveled only a few times in her life, and never without trepidation. The deeper she ventured into the ancient heart of Elaria, the more the air seemed to thrum with unseen magic. Vines coiled like serpents around twisted trunks, and the flowers that bloomed in this part of the forest radiated a faint, ethereal glow. It was as if she were walking through a world untouched by time, preserved in the echoes of old songs and lingering enchantments.

But the beauty did little to ease her unease. Every step was heavy with anticipation and an awareness that she was entering a domain not entirely welcoming to her kind. Her heart beat faster, but she forced herself to keep moving, knowing what was at stake.

At last, she arrived at a great hollow oak, its bark shimmering faintly in the dim light. The tree marked the threshold to the Fae Court—a place both tangible and elusive, where the boundary between the physical and the magical world blurred. As she approached, two sentries emerged from the shadows, their expressions cold and suspicious. Their eyes, golden and unblinking, scrutinized Lira with a disdain that sent a chill down her spine.

"Lira of Elaria," one of them intoned, his voice echoing as if spoken from a great distance. "State your purpose."

Lira bowed her head slightly, acknowledging their authority. "I seek an audience with Lady Kara," she replied, her voice steady despite her nerves.

The sentries exchanged a silent glance, communicating in the wordless way of their kind. One of them turned and disappeared into the hollow, while the other remained, his gaze never leaving Lira. She stood there, feeling the weight of the silence, the forest holding its breath around her.

Minutes passed, though it felt like an eternity, before the sentry returned and motioned for her to follow. She entered the hollow, the world shifting around her like a curtain being drawn aside. The air was cooler here, heavy with the scent of ancient wood and the faintest hint of wildflowers.

She emerged into the heart of the Fae Court, a sprawling grove of towering trees whose branches intertwined to form a natural canopy. The air was alive with whispers, and tiny motes of light drifted lazily through the shadows, like stars caught in a gentle breeze. At the center of the grove stood a great stone throne, carved with intricate patterns that seemed to move and shift when she looked at them too closely.

Seated upon the throne was Kara, the leader of the Fae. Her presence was commanding, every line of her slender form radiating a cold, fierce beauty. Her skin was pale and faintly luminescent, her hair cascading like liquid moonlight over her shoulders. But it was her eyes—sharp and blue as a winter sky—that held Lira's gaze and made her feel as if her soul were laid bare.

"Lira," Kara greeted, her voice cool and distant. She leaned forward slightly, her fingers drumming lightly on the arm of her throne. "You venture deep into our woods for someone who is not of our kind. Why?"

Lira took a deep breath and stepped forward, fighting the urge to shrink beneath the intensity of Kara's gaze. "Lady Kara," she began, her voice steady but laced with urgency. "Ironhold's machines are breaching the borders of Elaria. They're capturing spirits, corrupting them, and using their pain to fuel their creations. If we don't stand together—"

"'We?'" Kara interrupted, her voice tinged with amusement. "You speak as if you are one of us, child of men."

"I was raised in these woods," Lira countered, struggling to keep her tone respectful. "I've spent my life listening to the spirits, protecting them—"

"Protecting them?" Kara's laughter was soft and chilling, like the whisper of a cold wind. "How noble of you. And yet, you bear the blood of those who would destroy all they do not understand."

Lira felt her temper flare, but she forced herself to stay calm. "My blood doesn't define me," she said firmly. "My actions do. And right now, my only goal is to protect this forest and the spirits within it."

Kara's expression hardened, her eyes narrowing. "And you expect us to believe that you—*you*—can lead us in this fight? That we should risk our lives, our home, for a human's cause?"

"It's not just my cause," Lira insisted, her voice rising slightly. "Ironhold's machines won't stop at the borders of Elaria. If they're not stopped, the corruption will spread, and this forest—*all* of it—will be consumed."

Kara was silent for a long moment, her gaze never leaving Lira's. It was as if she were weighing every word, every breath, and finding it all lacking. When she finally spoke, her voice was cold and final.

"We have endured the march of time, the rise and fall of empires," she said softly. "And we will endure this as well. The Fae do not interfere in the affairs of mortals. Our place is to watch and wait, not to fight alongside those who have forsaken their kin."

"But I haven't forsaken—" Lira began, but Kara cut her off with a raised hand.

"Enough," she said, her voice sharp and commanding. "You have said your piece, Lira of Elaria. But you will find no allies here."

Lira felt a knot tighten in her chest, a mixture of frustration and despair. She had known convincing Kara wouldn't be easy, but she hadn't expected the wall of distrust to be so impenetrable.

"Lady Kara," she said, her voice quieter now, almost pleading. "I understand your distrust of humans. But this isn't just about our history—it's about our future. If we don't act now, there won't be a future left for any of us."

Kara's eyes softened slightly, but her expression remained resolute. "You speak of the future as if you understand it," she said quietly. "But you are still so young, so... mortal."

Lira opened her mouth to respond, but the words died on her lips. She realized then that no amount of reasoning or pleading would sway Kara's heart, not when centuries of mistrust and betrayal weighed so heavily upon it.

"I... see," Lira said finally, her voice barely a whisper. She bowed her head, acknowledging the Fae leader's authority, even as her heart ached with the sting of rejection. "Thank you for hearing me."

Kara inclined her head slightly, a gesture of distant courtesy. "Go now, child of men," she said softly. "And remember—if you bring war to our doorstep, it is not the Fae who will bear the cost."

Lira turned and left the grove, the shadows of the Fae Court closing in behind her like a final curtain. As she walked away, the whispers of the forest seemed quieter than before, as if mourning the fragile alliance that had never been.

Lira made her way back to Elder Ashen's grove, her heart heavy with the sting of rejection. Each step seemed to weigh more than the last, her thoughts circling back to the coldness in Kara's eyes, the finality of her words. The whispers of the spirits that usually surrounded her were distant, almost disinterested, as if mirroring her own doubts.

When she reached the grove, the air seemed stiller than usual. Elder Ashen stood in the center, his great branches stretching out like a protective canopy over the ancient clearing. Sunlight filtered through the leaves, casting dappled shadows on the ground. It was a place of refuge, a place of wisdom—yet in this moment, even the comfort of the familiar felt distant.

"Elder," Lira called softly, her voice thin and worn.

The great oak groaned in response, his deep voice resonating through the roots and into the very earth beneath her feet. "Child of the forest," Elder Ashen greeted, his tone laced with a softness that seemed to sense her turmoil. "You return with a troubled heart."

Lira approached slowly, placing her hand against his trunk as she had done so many times before. The rough texture of the bark felt steady, reassuring in its solidity. "I failed," she admitted, her voice catching. "Kara wouldn't listen. She won't join us."

Elder Ashen was silent for a long moment, his branches swaying gently in the breeze. When he spoke again, his voice carried a note of weary understanding. "The Fae are a proud and ancient people," he said. "Their trust is not easily given, nor quickly regained."

"I thought… I thought I could make her see," Lira murmured, her fingers tracing the deep grooves in Ashen's bark. "But all she could see was my humanity. She didn't trust me, and now

I don't know how to convince anyone else to fight alongside us."

The old tree spirit's branches creaked, as if contemplating her words. "You bear the burden of both worlds," he said softly. "It is no easy thing to walk between them."

Lira closed her eyes, leaning her forehead against the rough surface of the tree. "What if I can't do this?" she whispered, the weight of her self-doubt pressing down like a heavy fog. "What if I can't unite them? The Fae, the spirits… even the humans who might still care?"

Elder Ashen's voice was a low murmur, like the distant rumble of thunder. "Long ago, there was a pact between humans and spirits," he began, his tone taking on the cadence of an old storyteller. "A pact forged in a time when both sides recognized their need for one another."

Lira listened quietly, the words drawing her back to the stories she had heard as a child, tales of the Sacred Pact that once bound the forest and its people together. But those stories had always felt distant—mythical, almost dreamlike.

"What happened to it?" she asked, her voice barely above a whisper.

"Mistrust," Elder Ashen replied, his branches sighing with the weight of memories. "The humans feared what they did not understand, and the spirits grew wary of those who sought to tame what should be free. Greed followed, and ambition turned to betrayal. The Sacred Pact was broken, and with it, the balance was lost."

Lira felt a chill run down her spine, the echoes of the old story mingling with her own doubts. "But how do I rebuild something that's been broken for so long?" she asked, her voice tinged with frustration. "How do I bring them together when they only see the wounds of the past?"

Elder Ashen's branches rustled gently, a reminder of the passage of countless seasons. "Patience," he urged, his voice as steady as the earth beneath their feet. "Trust, once lost, cannot be reclaimed with words alone. It must be earned through action, through understanding."

"Patience..." Lira repeated, almost bitterly. "But Ironhold's machines are moving faster every day. The darkness is spreading, and I'm running out of time."

"The roots of a tree grow slowly, yet they hold the forest together," Elder Ashen said, his voice deep and resonant. "Rushing forward without understanding will only lead to more division. To unite the forest, you must learn to listen, even when the words are hard to hear."

Lira was silent, absorbing his words. She knew he was right—deep down, she had always known it. But knowing didn't make the waiting any easier, nor did it lessen the urgency of the threat Ironhold posed.

"Then what should I do?" she asked, her voice raw with the weight of her uncertainty.

Elder Ashen's leaves rustled softly, as if offering comfort. "Continue to reach out," he advised. "Show them through your actions that you are not merely human, but a guardian of this forest. Let your deeds speak where your words cannot."

Lira lifted her head, looking up at the great oak with renewed determination. "I won't give up," she said quietly, more to herself than to him. "I'll find a way."

"That is all we can ask of ourselves," Elder Ashen replied. "To keep seeking the path, even when it is hidden in shadow."

Lira took a deep breath, feeling the air around her grow warmer, more alive. The grove seemed to pulse with quiet strength, and she let it fill her, pushing back the lingering doubt.

"Thank you, Elder," she murmured, her voice steadier now.

"Go now, child," Elder Ashen said gently. "And remember—darkness may spread, but even the smallest spark can drive it away."

Lira nodded, a small, determined smile tugging at the corner of her lips. She turned and left the grove, her steps lighter than before, the weight of failure no longer dragging her down. There was still so much she didn't know, so many obstacles to overcome—but she would face them, one step at a time.

As she walked away, the whispers of the spirits grew stronger, their voices mingling with the rustling of leaves and the distant murmur of a river. Lira listened to them, not with impatience or frustration, but with a newfound sense of purpose.

She would not give up—not now, not ever. She would find a way to bridge the divide, to bring the forest's factions together. And no matter how long it took, she would earn their trust.

One step at a time.

Lira left the sanctuary of Elder Ashen's grove, the weight of her mission pressing down on her like a heavy mantle. As she walked through the ancient pathways of Elaria, the trees seemed to close in around her, their branches whispering in the soft breeze. There was a melancholy to the wind, a low murmur that carried the echoes of her earlier conversation with Kara and Elder Ashen's warnings.

She moved with purpose, her eyes ahead, but her mind drifted back to the cold finality of Kara's rejection. The memory of the Fae leader's disdainful gaze lingered like a bitter taste. *She didn't see me,* Lira thought, frustration knotting in her chest. *She only saw my blood.*

Despite the setback, Lira's resolve had not wavered; in fact, it had sharpened. Elder Ashen's words had planted a seed of understanding within her, one that spoke of patience and of the slow, deliberate growth of trust. Kara's rejection had stung deeply, but it was also a reminder of the ancient wounds that still festered between the Fae and humanity. Wounds that would not heal quickly, or easily.

The path before her twisted and turned, leading her back toward the forest's edge. It was a route she had taken many times, but today it felt different—longer, heavier, as if the weight of her thoughts was slowing her steps. Every leaf that fluttered down from the canopy seemed like a silent reminder of what was at stake.

"If the Fae won't stand with us," she muttered under her breath, "then I have to find another way."

A spirit creature darted across her path, a small, luminous fox-like creature that paused to watch her with curious eyes. Lira crouched down, her voice gentle. "What is it, little one?" she asked, extending her hand.

The creature tilted its head, its silver eyes reflecting the light of the forest. It was one of the lesser spirits, shy and often hidden, but its presence now felt like a silent acknowledgment of her resolve. It nudged her hand briefly before disappearing into the underbrush, a small gesture of support in a world that seemed increasingly divided.

As she continued her journey, the trees began to thin, the dense heart of the forest giving way to the more familiar woods near the border. Lira felt a pang of sadness as she left the depths of Elaria, the sanctuary of the grove fading behind her like a distant memory. She knew the weight of her task—bringing together the disparate forces of the forest, the Fae, the spirits, and whatever human allies she could find—would only grow heavier as she moved forward.

But as she neared the edge of the forest, her sadness transformed into determination. Elder Ashen's words replayed in her mind, a steady rhythm that kept her fears at bay. "The roots of a tree grow slowly, yet they hold the forest together," he had said. She knew now that unity wouldn't come from rushing or forcing others to see her way. It had to come from building trust, piece by piece.

As she reached the border, a familiar voice called out from the shadows, startling her. "Lira," Farael's voice carried a hint of reproach. The mist-wolf emerged from the shadows, his eyes narrowing as he studied her. "You're pushing yourself too hard."

"I have to," Lira replied, straightening her shoulders. "There isn't time to rest."

Farael's form shimmered slightly as he moved closer, the mist around him swirling like restless smoke. "Kara refused you, didn't she?" he asked, though his tone suggested he already knew the answer.

"Yes," Lira admitted, unable to hide the frustration in her voice. "She wouldn't listen. She's too focused on the past to see what's at risk now."

Farael sighed, the sound like leaves rustling in a mournful wind. "The Fae are old, Lira. Old and cautious. They've survived this long by staying out of human affairs."

"But this isn't just a human affair," Lira argued, her voice rising slightly. "It's about the forest, the spirits—everything. If Ironhold isn't stopped, it won't matter how cautious the Fae are. They'll lose everything, too."

The spirit creature met her gaze, his eyes piercing and ancient. "You believe in this path, even knowing it may lead to more pain?"

"I do," Lira replied, her voice steady. "Because doing nothing will only lead to more pain in the end. I have to try."

Farael was silent for a long moment, his form shifting slightly as if caught in an unseen breeze. "Then I will continue to watch over you," he said finally, his voice softening. "But be careful, Guardian. You bear a heavy burden, and you are not invincible."

Lira nodded, appreciating the spirit's concern even as she steeled herself for what lay ahead. "I know," she replied quietly. "But I'm not alone."

With those words, she turned and walked on, her pace more determined than before. She felt the eyes of the forest on her, watching, judging, waiting to see if she would falter. But she wouldn't. Not now.

As she reached the forest's edge, the sun dipped lower, casting long shadows across the path. The distant rumble of Ironhold's machines echoed faintly through the trees, a reminder of the threat looming ever closer. Lira paused for a moment, looking back at the woods that had been her home for as long as she could remember.

"I'll find a way," she murmured, her voice barely audible. "For the forest, for the spirits… for everyone."

The wind carried her words through the trees, a soft promise whispered to the ancient roots beneath her feet. Lira knew the road ahead would be fraught with challenges, with old mistrusts and new dangers, but she also knew that she couldn't allow fear to stop her.

So she continued forward, each step a silent vow to herself and to the forest she had sworn to protect. And as she left the shelter of the woods, the determination in her heart burned brighter, like a beacon in the gathering dusk.

Chapter 5
The Fae's Refusal

Lira approached the ancient hollow oak that marked the entrance to the Fae Court, its bark shimmering faintly in the soft light that filtered through the dense canopy. She took a steadying breath, her hand brushing against the smooth surface of the tree. The entrance opened without a sound, as if the tree itself had sensed her presence, and she stepped inside, feeling the air change—cooler, sharper, and alive with the hum of magic.

She emerged into a vast, open grove, surrounded by towering trees whose branches intertwined to form a natural canopy above. Motes of light drifted lazily through the air like tiny, luminescent fireflies. At the center of the grove stood a great stone throne, its surface carved with intricate patterns that seemed to move and shift when viewed from the corner of her eye.

Seated upon the throne was Lady Kara, the leader of the Fae. She was a commanding presence, her form elegant and ethereal. Her skin was pale and luminescent, her hair flowing like silver threads over her shoulders. But it was her eyes that held Lira's gaze—sharp and unyielding, like the winter sky.

"Lira of Elaria," Kara's voice rang out, clear and cold. "What brings you to our court?"

Lira bowed her head slightly, trying to mask her nerves. "Lady Kara," she began, choosing her words carefully. "I come to you seeking an alliance, a way to join forces against a common threat."

"An alliance?" Kara's eyebrow arched slightly, but her expression remained impassive. "And what threat would be so dire that you seek the aid of the Fae?"

"Ironhold," Lira replied, her voice steady despite the tension coiling within her. "Their machines are advancing into the forest, capturing spirits and corrupting them. They're using pain and dark magic to fuel their creations. If we don't stop them, the balance of Elaria will be lost."

Kara was silent for a long moment, her eyes studying Lira with an intensity that made her feel as though every secret she held was laid bare. "You speak of balance," Kara said finally, her tone edged with something akin to amusement. "As if you understand it."

Lira swallowed, trying to keep her composure. "I may not understand everything," she admitted, "but I know that Ironhold's actions are a threat to all of us—to the forest, to the spirits, and to your people as well. If we don't act, there will be nothing left to protect."

"You are bold," Kara observed, her voice soft but icy. "Bold and… perhaps, naïve."

"I'm not being naïve," Lira insisted, taking a step forward, her voice growing more urgent. "I've seen what Ironhold is doing. I've felt the pain of the spirits as their magic is twisted and consumed. If we don't stand together, we won't stand a chance."

Kara's eyes narrowed, and she leaned forward slightly, her fingers tapping lightly on the arm of her throne. "And why should we, the Fae, trust a human's words?" she asked, her voice laced with a cold edge. "Why should we risk our lives for a cause led by those who have betrayed us before?"

Lira felt a chill run down her spine, but she forced herself to meet Kara's gaze. "I was raised in these woods," she said firmly. "I've spent my life listening to the whispers of the forest and learning from the spirits. I may be human, but my loyalty is to Elaria, to the balance that sustains us all."

Kara's expression remained unreadable. "Loyalty," she repeated, as if testing the word. "You speak of loyalty, and yet your kind has broken every promise it has ever made to us. You speak of trust, and yet trust is a luxury the Fae can no longer afford."

"That was a different time," Lira argued, desperation creeping into her voice. "The humans who made those mistakes are long gone. I'm not asking you to forget the past, but to look to the future—"

"The future?" Kara interrupted, her voice sharper now. "The future you speak of is built on the ruins of our past. You ask me to trust you, a human, to lead us against Ironhold. Do you not see the irony in your request?"

Lira's heart sank, and she felt her resolve waver. She had expected resistance, but not this—this cold, unyielding wall of mistrust. "I'm not asking you to trust me blindly," she said, her voice barely more than a whisper. "I'm asking you to trust in what we all stand to lose if we do nothing."

Kara rose from her throne, her movements graceful but deliberate, like the flowing of water turning to ice. She stepped down from the stone platform, her eyes never leaving Lira's. "You come to my court, speaking of loss and balance, as if these are things you understand," she said softly, her tone almost pitying. "But you are still so young, so… mortal."

"I'm trying to protect the forest," Lira replied, her voice trembling slightly. "To protect everything that lives here."

"And yet," Kara said, her voice growing colder, "you carry the blood of those who nearly destroyed us centuries ago. Your intentions may be noble, Lira of Elaria, but intentions are not enough."

"What would be enough, then?" Lira demanded, the frustration breaking through her restraint. "What would it take for you to believe in something other than old wounds and ancient grudges?"

Kara's expression hardened, and her eyes flashed with a dangerous light. "You presume much, child," she said, her voice like ice cracking beneath the weight of winter's first frost. "You presume to ask the Fae to risk their lives for your cause, without understanding the cost."

Lira felt a knot tighten in her chest, a mixture of frustration and despair. She had come here seeking an ally, but all she had found was a reminder of the distance between them. "Then tell me," she said softly, her voice almost pleading. "Tell me what it would take to earn your trust."

Kara was silent for a long moment, her gaze piercing. "Trust is not something you can earn with words," she said finally, her voice almost a whisper. "Nor is it something given lightly. You speak of fighting Ironhold, of protecting the forest, but you cannot protect what you do not understand."

Lira took a deep breath, trying to keep her voice steady. "Then teach me," she said, her voice firm despite the fear gnawing at her heart. "Show me what I don't understand."

Kara's expression softened, but only slightly. "You are bold," she repeated quietly. "And boldness is not without merit. But boldness alone will not save you."

Lira lowered her gaze, feeling the weight of Kara's words like a heavy stone in her chest. She had failed. She had come seeking an alliance, but all she had found was rejection.

"Thank you for hearing me, Lady Kara," she said softly, her voice tinged with defeat.

"Go now, child of men," Kara replied, her voice cold and distant once more. "And remember—if you bring war to our doorstep, it is not the Fae who will bear the cost."

Lira bowed her head, turning away from the throne and walking back towards the entrance of the grove. As she left the Fae Court, she felt the whispers of the forest grow quieter, as if even the trees were mourning the fragile alliance that had never been.

She had failed, and with every step she took away from the grove, the weight of that failure pressed down on her, leaving her wondering if she was truly capable of leading anyone at all.

Lira walked aimlessly through the dense underbrush of Elaria, the rejection replaying in her mind like an unwelcome echo. The sunlight filtering through the thick canopy above felt duller, and the normally vibrant greens of the forest seemed muted to her eyes. She stopped occasionally, pressing her palm against the trunks of the ancient trees, listening for the comforting whispers that usually surrounded her. But the forest seemed quieter today, its voice barely more than a murmur.

The coldness in Kara's words haunted her. *Naïve… human… mortal.* Lira's hands trembled at the memory, the anger she felt turning inward now, laced with doubt.

"What if she's right?" Lira whispered to the trees, her voice barely audible. "What if I'm just rushing into this, desperate to fix things that can't be mended?"

She waited, half-expecting some sign from the forest—an affirming whisper, a breeze that spoke of reassurance. But there was nothing but silence and the distant rustle of leaves. Lira took a deep breath, forcing herself to continue walking. She felt lost, not just in the forest, but within herself.

Her feet carried her instinctively towards a familiar place, a quiet stream that ran through the heart of the forest. The water was clear and gentle, the stream's flow creating soft ripples that sparkled in the patches of sunlight. Lira knelt by the water's edge, her reflection staring back at her, the same face she had always known yet now appearing foreign in her own eyes.

She cupped some water in her hands, letting it trickle through her fingers, watching the droplets return to the stream. As she did, she heard the faintest whisper—gentle and hesitant, as if the spirits themselves were unsure of what to say.

Patience, child... the voice seemed to say.

Lira's heart ached at the sound, recognizing the echo of Elder Ashen's teachings. She closed her eyes, trying to remember his words from their last conversation. "Patience isn't inaction," she murmured, almost as if reciting a mantra. "It's the wisdom to act at the right moment."

But when was the right moment? And how would she know if she was waiting too long?

"Was I wrong to push so hard?" Lira asked aloud, her voice trembling slightly. She felt the familiar sting of tears at the corners of her eyes, and she blinked them away, her fists clenching at her sides. "Or am I just too afraid of failing?"

For a long time, there was no response, only the soft gurgling of the stream and the distant calls of birds. Lira buried her face in her hands, her shoulders trembling with the weight of uncertainty. She was supposed to be a guardian, a protector of the forest, but right now she felt more like a lost child.

"Lira," a voice spoke softly, not from the trees but behind her.

Lira looked up, startled, and turned to see Bryn, one of the forest spirits she had known since childhood. Bryn was a gentle soul, their form barely more substantial than mist, with eyes like pools of moonlight. They stepped closer, their voice hesitant.

"Bryn," Lira greeted, trying to mask the turmoil in her voice. "What are you doing here?"

"I sensed your sorrow," Bryn replied, their voice like a gentle breeze. "The forest has grown restless with it."

Lira let out a shaky breath. "I… I went to the Fae Court," she admitted. "I tried to convince them to join us, but they refused. Lady Kara—she doesn't trust me. She doesn't trust *humans*."

Bryn watched her with a quiet patience. "Trust is not easily given," they said softly. "Especially not by those who have been wounded before."

"I know that," Lira said, frustration creeping into her voice. "But I just— I thought if I could show her what was at stake, she'd understand. That she'd *care* enough to help."

"And now?" Bryn asked, tilting their head slightly. "What do you intend to do now?"

Lira didn't have an answer, not one she could articulate. She felt trapped between the urgency of Ironhold's advance and the lingering echo of Kara's rejection. The Fae had seen her plea as a sign of weakness, and maybe they were right.

"I don't know," Lira admitted, her voice barely more than a whisper. "I thought I was doing the right thing, but now… I'm not so sure."

Bryn knelt beside her, their translucent form reflecting the dappled sunlight. "The Fae have lived in isolation for many centuries," they said gently. "To them, trust is a fragile thing, and you are an outsider to their pain."

"Then how am I supposed to convince them?" Lira asked, her voice breaking slightly. "How can I protect the forest if I can't even unite the people in it?"

"Perhaps the answer is not in grand alliances," Bryn suggested, their voice thoughtful. "Perhaps it is in the smaller acts of unity that you will find the strength you seek."

Lira frowned, trying to make sense of the words. "What do you mean?"

Bryn smiled faintly, their eyes reflecting the sunlight. "The whispers of the forest have not fallen silent," they said. "There are still spirits who watch and listen, waiting for a sign of hope. Perhaps, instead of seeking alliances from those who do not yet trust you, you should seek out those who are already open to your voice."

Lira looked down at the stream, watching the water flow gently over the rocks. Bryn's words made sense, in a way. She had been so focused on winning over the Fae, on creating a grand alliance, that she had ignored the smaller, quieter voices around her.

"Do you think it would be enough?" Lira asked softly, a hint of doubt lingering in her voice.

"Small acts of unity are like drops of water," Bryn replied. "One alone may seem insignificant, but many together can form a river that shapes the land."

Lira took a deep breath, feeling a flicker of hope stirring within her. Perhaps she had been looking at this all wrong. Perhaps the strength she needed wasn't in the alliances she couldn't forge, but in the spirits and friends she already had.

"Thank you, Bryn," she said quietly, her voice steadying. "You've given me a lot to think about."

Bryn inclined their head, their form shifting slightly in the breeze. "The forest is not yet lost, Lira," they said softly. "And neither are you."

Lira smiled faintly, feeling a sense of clarity begin to return. She still didn't have all the answers, but at least now she had a direction—a path to follow, even if it wasn't the one she had expected.

As she rose to her feet, she listened to the soft whispers of the forest, not as a distant murmur, but as a quiet chorus of hope. Perhaps she wasn't as alone as she had feared. Perhaps, even in rejection, there was a way forward.

Lira felt the weight of Kara's rejection linger, like the chill of a bitter wind. But as she moved deeper into the forest, following the old paths less traveled, that chill began to lift. Bryn's words echoed in her mind, urging her to seek out those who still had faith in the forest's voice—those who were distant from the politics and pain of old grudges.

She headed towards the northern groves, a place known to be home to the older spirits—those who lived away from the more populated parts of Elaria. These spirits were not part of the Fae Court, nor were they directly affected by Ironhold's immediate expansion. They existed quietly, living out their long lives in peace. But perhaps it was in their isolation that Lira could find hope.

The forest changed as she approached the northern groves. The trees here were older, their trunks wider and their branches sprawling like great arms that shielded the ground from the sky. Moss hung thickly, and the air felt cooler, untouched by the heat of the sun. Lira moved cautiously, her fingers brushing against the bark as she walked. The forest here felt different—more alive in a way that was harder to articulate.

"Elder Moira?" Lira called softly, her voice careful not to disturb the serene quiet. She waited, holding her breath, listening for the slightest response.

A moment passed, and then another. She began to wonder if Elder Moira was even here when the bark of the nearest tree shifted, revealing an old face, weathered and creased like the lines of a well-read book. The spirit's eyes were deep and dark, reflecting the wisdom of centuries.

"Lira of Elaria," the old spirit greeted, her voice slow and measured. "It has been many moons since you last sought me out. What brings you to these forgotten groves?"

"I… I came to ask for your guidance," Lira replied, bowing her head respectfully. "And your help, if you would give it."

Moira's branches creaked as she leaned closer, her ancient eyes narrowing slightly. "Help with what, child?"

Lira took a deep breath, steadying herself. "Ironhold is advancing further into the forest. Their machines are capturing and corrupting spirits. I tried to gain the Fae's support, but they refused me. They don't trust me, and I can't blame them. I'm human, after all."

"Ah," Moira murmured, her voice tinged with a faint sadness. "The Fae have long memories, and old wounds do not heal easily. But why come to us? We are not warriors, nor do we meddle in the affairs of the Fae or Ironhold."

"I know," Lira said, her voice softening. "But I believe that the strength of the forest isn't just in the Fae or in its power—it's in all of you. The older spirits, the forgotten ones, the quiet voices that are often overlooked."

Moira was silent for a moment, her expression contemplative. "You speak with conviction, Lira. But conviction alone is not enough."

"I know," Lira admitted, a hint of desperation in her voice. "But if there's anything I've learned, it's that alliances aren't built in grand gestures. They're built in the small moments of trust and understanding. And right now, I need to earn your trust, not by asking you to fight, but by listening to what you have to say."

Moira's eyes seemed to soften at Lira's words, her ancient face showing the barest hint of a smile. "You have learned some measure of humility, it seems," the old spirit remarked. "That is not an easy lesson for one so young."

"I'm trying," Lira replied, her voice barely above a whisper. "I'm trying to be the guardian that the forest needs, but I can't do it alone. I need to learn from those who came before me."

Moira let out a slow breath, her branches swaying gently in the breeze. "There are others who might be willing to listen to you," she said quietly. "Spirits who have lived in isolation, far from the reach of Ironhold's shadow. They are wary of change, but they may yet be swayed by your sincerity."

"Where can I find them?" Lira asked, her heart lifting with a cautious hope.

"Beyond the stone circle, in the oldest part of the grove," Moira replied. "Seek out the Willow Sisters. They are wise in their way, though they are often misunderstood by those who do not take the time to listen."

Lira nodded, bowing her head in gratitude. "Thank you, Elder Moira. I will do my best to earn their trust."

"Go, child," Moira said softly. "But remember this: trust is not won with words alone. It is won with actions that reflect the truth of one's heart."

Lira left the northern groves feeling lighter, the weight of rejection lifting slightly from her shoulders. She had not won over the Fae, but that did not mean she was alone. There were other spirits, other allies waiting to be found. And perhaps, in the quiet places of Elaria, there was a strength that had not yet been tested.

When she reached the stone circle, she found the Willow Sisters waiting—three ancient spirits whose forms were intertwined with the slender, graceful branches of willow trees. Their faces were serene, but their eyes were sharp, watching her with a mixture of curiosity and caution.

"Lira of Elaria," one of the sisters greeted, her voice as soft as a whispering breeze. "What brings you to our grove?"

Lira took a deep breath, feeling the old hesitation trying to creep back into her heart. But she pushed it aside, focusing on the resolve that had carried her this far. "I came to listen," she replied, her voice steady. "And to ask for your guidance."

The sisters exchanged glances, their branches swaying gently. "Few come to listen," another of the sisters remarked, her tone thoughtful. "Many come to speak, but not to listen."

"I'm not here to force anyone to act," Lira said quietly. "But if there's a way to protect this forest—our home—I want to learn it. Even if it takes time."

The third sister, who had been silent until now, let out a soft sigh. "Patience is a virtue rarely seen in those who are mortal," she said, her voice tinged with quiet amusement. "But perhaps there is more to you than meets the eye."

Lira smiled faintly, feeling her confidence return bit by bit. The path forward was still uncertain, but she was no longer standing still. She was moving, slowly but surely, towards a future that she was willing to fight for—not just with power, but with compassion and understanding.

It wasn't the grand alliance she had hoped for, but it was a start. And for now, that was enough.

Lira felt the weight of Kara's rejection linger, like the chill of a bitter wind. But as she moved deeper into the forest, following the old paths less traveled, that chill began to lift. Bryn's words echoed in her mind, urging her to seek out those who still had faith in the forest's voice—those who were distant from the politics and pain of old grudges.

She headed towards the northern groves, a place known to be home to the older spirits—those who lived away from the more populated parts of Elaria. These spirits were not part of the Fae Court, nor were they directly affected by Ironhold's immediate expansion. They existed quietly, living out their long lives in peace. But perhaps it was in their isolation that Lira could find hope.

The forest changed as she approached the northern groves. The trees here were older, their trunks wider and their branches sprawling like great arms that shielded the ground from the sky. Moss hung thickly, and the air felt cooler, untouched by the heat of the sun. Lira moved cautiously, her fingers brushing against the bark as she walked. The forest here felt different— more alive in a way that was harder to articulate.

"Elder Moira?" Lira called softly, her voice careful not to disturb the serene quiet. She waited, holding her breath, listening for the slightest response.

A moment passed, and then another. She began to wonder if Elder Moira was even here when the bark of the nearest tree shifted, revealing an old face, weathered and creased like the lines of a well-read book. The spirit's eyes were deep and dark, reflecting the wisdom of centuries.

"Lira of Elaria," the old spirit greeted, her voice slow and measured. "It has been many moons since you last sought me out. What brings you to these forgotten groves?"

"I… I came to ask for your guidance," Lira replied, bowing her head respectfully. "And your help, if you would give it."

Moira's branches creaked as she leaned closer, her ancient eyes narrowing slightly. "Help with what, child?"

Lira took a deep breath, steadying herself. "Ironhold is advancing further into the forest. Their machines are capturing and corrupting spirits. I tried to gain the Fae's support, but they refused me. They don't trust me, and I can't blame them. I'm human, after all."

"Ah," Moira murmured, her voice tinged with a faint sadness. "The Fae have long memories, and old wounds do not heal easily. But why come to us? We are not warriors, nor do we meddle in the affairs of the Fae or Ironhold."

"I know," Lira said, her voice softening. "But I believe that the strength of the forest isn't just in the Fae or in its power—it's in all of you. The older spirits, the forgotten ones, the quiet voices that are often overlooked."

Moira was silent for a moment, her expression contemplative. "You speak with conviction, Lira. But conviction alone is not enough."

"I know," Lira admitted, a hint of desperation in her voice. "But if there's anything I've learned, it's that alliances aren't built in grand gestures. They're built in the small moments of trust and understanding. And right now, I need to earn your trust, not by asking you to fight, but by listening to what you have to say."

Moira's eyes seemed to soften at Lira's words, her ancient face showing the barest hint of a smile. "You have learned some measure of humility, it seems," the old spirit remarked. "That is not an easy lesson for one so young."

"I'm trying," Lira replied, her voice barely above a whisper. "I'm trying to be the guardian that the forest needs, but I can't do it alone. I need to learn from those who came before me."

Moira let out a slow breath, her branches swaying gently in the breeze. "There are others who might be willing to listen to you," she said quietly. "Spirits who have lived in isolation, far from the reach of Ironhold's shadow. They are wary of change, but they may yet be swayed by your sincerity."

"Where can I find them?" Lira asked, her heart lifting with a cautious hope.

"Beyond the stone circle, in the oldest part of the grove," Moira replied. "Seek out the Willow Sisters. They are wise in their way, though they are often misunderstood by those who do not take the time to listen."

Lira nodded, bowing her head in gratitude. "Thank you, Elder Moira. I will do my best to earn their trust."

"Go, child," Moira said softly. "But remember this: trust is not won with words alone. It is won with actions that reflect the truth of one's heart."

Lira left the northern groves feeling lighter, the weight of rejection lifting slightly from her shoulders. She had not won over the Fae, but that did not mean she was alone. There were other spirits, other allies waiting to be found. And perhaps, in the quiet places of Elaria, there was a strength that had not yet been tested.

When she reached the stone circle, she found the Willow Sisters waiting—three ancient spirits whose forms were intertwined with the slender, graceful branches of willow trees. Their faces were serene, but their eyes were sharp, watching her with a mixture of curiosity and caution.

"Lira of Elaria," one of the sisters greeted, her voice as soft as a whispering breeze. "What brings you to our grove?"

Lira took a deep breath, feeling the old hesitation trying to creep back into her heart. But she pushed it aside, focusing on the resolve that had carried her this far. "I came to listen," she replied, her voice steady. "And to ask for your guidance."

The sisters exchanged glances, their branches swaying gently. "Few come to listen," another of the sisters remarked, her tone thoughtful. "Many come to speak, but not to listen."

"I'm not here to force anyone to act," Lira said quietly. "But if there's a way to protect this forest—our home—I want to learn it. Even if it takes time."

The third sister, who had been silent until now, let out a soft sigh. "Patience is a virtue rarely seen in those who are mortal," she said, her voice tinged with quiet amusement. "But perhaps there is more to you than meets the eye."

Lira smiled faintly, feeling her confidence return bit by bit. The path forward was still uncertain, but she was no longer standing still. She was moving, slowly but surely, towards a future that she was willing to fight for—not just with power, but with compassion and understanding.

It wasn't the grand alliance she had hoped for, but it was a start. And for now, that was enough.

Chapter 6
Gathering the Lost

The Wild Ones were as much a part of Elaria as the roots of the ancient oaks, but they lived in the deep, hidden places where even the boldest spirits dared not wander. Lira had only heard whispers of them—ancient beings of immense power and mystery, creatures that held the old magic of the forest within their very essence. They were as wild as the name suggested, unbound by the rules of men or spirits, answering only to the rhythm of the land itself.

Lira ventured deeper into the forest, her footsteps guided by instinct and the faint, almost inaudible hum of ancient magic that seemed to pulse through the air. She had been walking for hours, and every part of her ached with the weight of doubt and exhaustion. But there was no turning back now. The Fae had rejected her plea, and while the spirits of the forest trusted her, their strength alone would not be enough. She needed the Wild Ones to stand with them.

She reached a secluded grove, the trees here older than any she had ever seen. Their trunks were massive, their branches twisted and gnarled, forming a canopy so dense that the sunlight struggled to break through. The air was thick with magic, a tangible energy that made the hair on the back of her neck stand on end.

"Hello?" she called, her voice trembling slightly despite her resolve. "I am Lira, guardian of Elaria. I seek an audience with the Wild Ones."

There was no answer, only the rustling of leaves and the distant call of a bird. Lira took a deep breath, trying to steady herself. She could feel eyes watching her from the shadows, an unsettling sensation that made her skin prickle.

"I know you're here," she continued, her voice firmer. "I need your help to protect this forest—to protect Elaria."

A low growl echoed through the grove, and Lira froze, her heart hammering in her chest. The shadows seemed to shift, and out of the darkness stepped a massive creature, its fur blending seamlessly with the shadows around it. It was unlike anything she had ever seen—a great wolf with eyes that glowed faintly like embers, its presence commanding and primal.

"Why do you disturb our slumber, child of men?" the creature rumbled, its voice deep and resonant. It did not move closer, but its gaze pinned her in place.

Lira swallowed hard, forcing herself to stand her ground. "I came because Elaria is in danger," she said, her voice clear despite the fear curling in her stomach. "Ironhold's machines are tearing the forest apart. Spirits are being captured and corrupted. And the Fae refuse to help."

The great wolf tilted its head, its eyes narrowing. "The Fae have always hidden behind their pride," it replied with a low snarl. "But their weakness is not our concern. The forest endures, as it always has."

"Not this time," Lira insisted, taking a step forward. "Ironhold's leaders are repeating the mistakes of the past. If we do nothing, Elaria will fall—just like it did during the Sundering."

The creature growled softly, its eyes flickering with something like recognition. "The Sundering," it murmured, almost as if the word itself carried a weight. "A name we do not speak lightly."

"I've seen the memories," Lira continued, her voice gaining strength. "The Obelisk showed me what happened—how humans broke the Sacred Pact, how they turned on the spirits. But that's not what I want. I'm not here to repeat history—I'm here to make things right."

The wolf studied her in silence, its gaze intense and piercing. Lira felt a cold sweat break out on the back of her neck, but she met its gaze, refusing to look away. Finally, the creature spoke.

"Words are easy to speak, but hard to trust," it said, its tone laced with a quiet warning. "The Wild Ones do not meddle in the affairs of humans. We are the keepers of the old ways, bound to the land and its balance."

"I understand," Lira replied, her voice soft but resolute. "But I'm not asking you to fight for me—I'm asking you to fight for Elaria. To fight for the balance that Ironhold threatens to destroy."

The wolf tilted its head, considering her words. "And if we refuse?" it asked, its voice a low rumble.

Lira took a deep breath, her fingers curling into fists at her sides. "Then I'll fight alone," she said firmly. "I'll do whatever it takes to protect this forest, even if it costs me everything."

There was a long, heavy silence, broken only by the faint rustling of leaves and the distant hum of ancient magic. Lira held her breath, waiting for the creature's response, her heart pounding in her chest.

After what felt like an eternity, the wolf let out a low, rumbling laugh. "You are bold, human," it said, a hint of amusement in its voice. "And perhaps a little foolish. But there is something in your eyes... something familiar."

Lira exhaled slowly, relief mingling with the lingering tension. "Will you help us?" she asked, her voice almost a whisper.

The wolf regarded her for a moment longer, then inclined its head. "We will not fight *for* you," it said, its tone still cautious. "But we will not stand by and watch Elaria fall, either. If you are true to your word, then the Wild Ones will lend their strength to protect the balance."

"Thank you," Lira replied, her voice filled with gratitude.

"Do not thank us yet," the wolf warned. "Your path is fraught with danger, and not all of the Wild Ones share my caution. Some would sooner see the world burn than risk betrayal again."

"I'll prove myself," Lira promised, determination burning in her eyes.

The wolf nodded once, its form beginning to fade into the shadows. "We shall see," it said softly, its voice lingering even as its presence vanished. "We shall see."

As the creature disappeared, Lira felt the tension leave her shoulders, replaced by a cautious hope. It wasn't a victory, not yet—but it was a step forward. The Wild Ones had agreed to help, and that meant there was still a chance to save Elaria.

She turned and made her way back through the forest, the whispers of the ancient magic still lingering in the air. Her path was clearer now, and her resolve stronger than ever. No matter the cost, she would fight to preserve the balance of Elaria.

And for the first time in a long while, she didn't feel so alone.

Lira moved silently through the underbrush, her senses attuned to the rustle of leaves and the subtle movements of small creatures in the twilight. The forest around her was quiet, save for the distant calls of night birds and the occasional whisper of the wind. She had been scouting the border between Elaria and Ironhold's expanding reach for days now, gathering what little information she could on the invaders' movements and the changes in the forest's magic.

She paused near a large, ancient oak, her fingers brushing against its bark. Closing her eyes, she listened to the whispers of the tree, the low murmur of ancient roots sharing news of trespassers. But amidst the usual hum of the forest, there was something else—a presence, nearby and unfamiliar. Someone was watching her.

Lira's eyes snapped open, her hand moving instinctively to the small dagger she carried. "Show yourself," she called softly, her voice firm but measured. "I know you're there."

There was a rustling from the shadows, and a figure stepped cautiously into the faint moonlight. It was a young man, his dark coat marked with the symbols of Ironhold, and his face half-concealed by the hood he wore. Lira's grip on the dagger tightened as she recognized him—Fenn, the engineer she had seen in the clearing weeks ago.

"You," Lira said, her voice low and wary.

Fenn raised his hands slightly, a gesture of peace. "Please," he said, his voice barely above a whisper. "I just want to talk."

Lira didn't lower her dagger, her eyes narrowing. "Why should I trust you? You're one of them."

Fenn hesitated, his gaze shifting to the ground before he met her eyes again. "I know," he admitted. "And I know you have every reason not to trust me. But... I came because I need your help. And because I want to help you."

"Help me?" Lira repeated, incredulity lacing her voice. "You expect me to believe that? After everything your people have done?"

Fenn took a cautious step forward, his eyes earnest. "I didn't know," he said quietly, his voice laced with regret. "I didn't know what the engines were really doing to the spirits until… until you showed me."

Lira's grip on the dagger loosened slightly, but she didn't lower it. "You didn't know?" she echoed, her tone skeptical. "Or you just didn't want to see?"

Fenn's face tightened at her words, but he didn't look away. "Maybe both," he admitted. "But I know now. I found Harrow's journals, the ones that told the truth about the pact—about the betrayal. And I can't keep pretending everything we're doing is for progress, or that it's right."

Lira searched his face for any sign of deception, but all she saw was a young man struggling with his own guilt and doubt. Still, she couldn't let her guard down—not yet. "So why come to me?" she asked, her voice cold. "What do you want?"

"I want to stop Ironhold's machines," Fenn replied, his voice firm despite the fear she could see in his eyes. "I want to make this right, if I can. I have information—about the new designs, about their weaknesses. I thought… if I could give you that, maybe you could use it to protect the forest."

Lira frowned, her mind racing. If he was telling the truth, this information could be invaluable. But there was still a nagging voice at the back of her mind, warning her to be cautious. She couldn't afford to be betrayed—not when so much was at stake.

"You could be leading me into a trap," she said, her tone accusatory. "How do I know this isn't some trick?"

Fenn's expression softened, and for a moment, Lira saw the uncertainty in his eyes—fear, yes, but also a flicker of hope. "You don't," he replied honestly. "But I'm not here on the Chancellor's orders, and I didn't bring anyone with me. If I was lying, I wouldn't have come alone."

Lira studied him, weighing his words. There was a sincerity in his voice that made her want to believe him, but trust was a fragile thing, and she had seen too many betrayals to let her guard down easily.

"What do you get out of this?" she asked finally, her voice sharper than she intended. "Why risk everything to help me?"

Fenn hesitated, his eyes lowering as if he were searching for the right words. "I don't know if I can make up for what I've done," he admitted quietly. "Or for what my people have done. But I can't just stand by and watch the forest die. Not after what I've seen. Not after what I've read."

He looked up, meeting her gaze. "You said the spirits were hurting, and I didn't believe you. But now... I hear them, too. I feel them. And I can't ignore it anymore."

Lira's breath caught at his words, the memories of her own connection to the spirits resurfacing. She could sense his struggle, the weight of his doubts, and the guilt that seemed to hang over him like a shadow. For a long moment, neither of them spoke, the silence heavy with unspoken fears and lingering distrust.

Finally, Lira lowered her dagger, though she didn't fully relax. "If you're lying to me..." she began, her voice carrying a quiet threat.

"I'm not," Fenn interrupted, his tone urgent. "I swear it. Just... let me help. Let me prove it."

Lira stared at him for a moment longer before she finally nodded, though the tension in her shoulders remained. "Alright," she said slowly. "Tell me what you know."

Fenn let out a breath he hadn't realized he was holding, and he stepped closer, pulling a worn map from his coat. He spread it out on the ground between them, pointing to a series of marks near the forest's border.

"These are the locations of the newer machines," he explained, his voice steady despite the tremor in his hands. "The core systems are vulnerable to overload if the containment runes are disrupted—here and here." He pointed to specific points on the sketches. "But it won't be easy. The runes are reinforced daily, and the guards—"

Lira listened closely, her skepticism slowly giving way to cautious curiosity. The details he provided were more than she expected, and his knowledge of the machines' workings seemed genuine. She felt the beginnings of a plan forming in her mind, a plan that hinged on the possibility that Fenn was telling the truth.

When he finished, he looked up at her, his expression one of quiet desperation. "Does that help?" he asked, his voice almost a whisper.

Lira didn't answer immediately. Instead, she studied him one last time, searching his face for any trace of deceit. But all she saw was a young man trying to make sense of the choices he had made—and the consequences he was now trying to atone for.

"It's a start," she replied finally, her voice cautious but not unkind. "But if you want to help, you have to follow my lead. No more secrets, no more half-truths."

Fenn nodded, relief evident in his eyes. "I understand," he said quietly.

Lira glanced at the map again, the weight of the alliance they had just forged settling over her like a fragile bridge between two worlds. There was still so much she didn't know about him, and so much he didn't know about her. But for now, it was enough.

"Then let's not waste time," she said, folding the map and tucking it into her belt. "We have a forest to protect."

The forest seemed to hold its breath as Fenn gathered up his belongings, his fingers trembling slightly as he rolled up the worn map he had shown Lira. His expression was one of tense determination, a reflection of the inner battle raging within him.

Lira stood a few paces away, her arms crossed, watching his every movement with wary eyes.

Fenn cleared his throat, breaking the heavy silence between them. "I'll head back before anyone notices I'm gone," he said, his voice quiet but steady. He glanced up at her, searching for a sign that she believed him, that she trusted him even a little. But Lira's expression was guarded, her green eyes sharp and unreadable.

She nodded curtly, the tension between them lingering like the mist that clung to the trees. "Be careful," she said, her voice more of a command than a suggestion. "If Ironhold suspects you're working against them…"

"I know," Fenn replied, cutting her off. He tucked the map into his coat and straightened, trying to project more confidence than he felt. "I'll be careful."

For a moment, neither of them spoke. The quiet of the forest seemed to press in on them, amplifying every rustle of leaves, every distant call of an owl. Fenn shifted awkwardly, unsure of what else to say. He had come here with the hope of forging an alliance, but he knew it was a fragile one at best—a bridge built on uneasy trust and shared necessity.

Lira's voice cut through the silence, sharp and direct. "Why are you really doing this?" she asked, her gaze piercing. "What do you hope to gain?"

Fenn met her eyes, feeling the weight of her question settle heavily on his shoulders. He had asked himself the same thing countless times, trying to untangle the knots of guilt and doubt that seemed to grow tighter with every step he took. "I'm doing this because I can't ignore what I've seen," he replied, his voice quieter now. "Because pretending everything is fine isn't an option anymore."

Lira studied him, searching his face for any hint of deception. She wasn't ready to trust him completely—not yet. But there was something in his eyes, something genuine and almost… lost. It reminded her of her own doubts and fears, of the moments when she had questioned her place in this ancient battle between the forest and those who sought to control it.

"You might be the key," she murmured, more to herself than to him.

Fenn frowned slightly. "Key to what?"

"To understanding Ironhold's strategy," Lira replied, her voice firm. "To finding a way to stop them before they destroy everything."

He let out a slow breath, relief mingling with the weight of responsibility. "I want to help," he said softly. "But I'm not sure if I'm strong enough to face what's coming."

Lira's expression softened, if only slightly. She understood that feeling all too well—the fear of being unprepared, of not knowing if you could endure the path ahead. But she had learned to push through that fear, to find strength in the uncertainty.

"We don't have a choice," she said, her voice steady. "The forest is counting on us—on all of us."

Fenn nodded, swallowing hard. He could feel the enormity of what lay ahead pressing down on him, but he also felt a strange sense of resolve. This alliance, however uneasy, was a chance to make things right—a chance he couldn't afford to waste.

"I'll find a way to get more information," he promised, his voice low but determined. "I'll keep you informed about any changes or new developments in Ironhold."

"Good," Lira replied, her tone brisk. "But don't take unnecessary risks. If they catch you…"

"I know," Fenn said quickly, cutting her off again. He hesitated, then added, "Thank you… for giving me a chance."

Lira didn't respond immediately. She could see the sincerity in his eyes, but trust was not something she could give freely—not after everything she had seen, everything she had lost. Still, she nodded, acknowledging his words with a small, almost imperceptible inclination of her head.

"Don't make me regret it," she said quietly.

Fenn offered a faint, hesitant smile. "I won't," he replied, though the uncertainty in his voice was impossible to ignore. With one last look at Lira, he turned and disappeared into the trees, the darkness swallowing him up as if he were just another shadow moving through the night.

Lira stood there for a moment longer, listening to the sounds of the forest around her. The whispers of the spirits were faint but present, a reminder of the ever-watchful eyes that observed her every move. She felt a pang of unease, a gnawing worry that she had made a mistake in trusting Fenn. But there was also a spark of hope—an inkling that he might be the key to understanding Ironhold's plans and preventing the coming disaster.

"Elder Ashen," she murmured, closing her eyes and placing a hand against the rough bark of the ancient oak beside her. "Did I do the right thing?"

The tree was silent for a long moment, and then a faint whisper brushed against her mind, like the sigh of a gentle breeze. *"Trust is a fragile thing,"* Elder Ashen's voice murmured, resonating through the wood and into her very soul. *"But without it, nothing grows."*

Lira opened her eyes, taking in the ancient grove around her. She could still feel the weight of the choices she had made pressing down on her, but she also felt a renewed sense of purpose. The path ahead was uncertain, and the alliance with Fenn was fraught with risk. But she couldn't afford to turn away from the possibility of understanding her enemy—or finding the key to saving Elaria.

She let out a slow breath, her fingers trailing along the grooves in the oak's bark. "I'll keep my guard up," she promised, both to herself and to the forest that had become her home. "But I won't turn away from the help I need."

The spirits' whispers grew softer, and the air around her seemed to calm, as if the forest itself had acknowledged her resolve. Lira turned away from the grove, her steps lighter but her heart still weighed down by uncertainty.

There were so many questions left unanswered, so many dangers yet unseen. But for the first time in a long while, Lira felt that she wasn't facing the darkness alone. And that, at least, was something to hold on to.

Chapter 7
Paths Unseen

Lira made her way carefully through the dense thicket, her boots sinking slightly into the mossy ground. The forest felt different here—older, more alive in a way that wasn't immediately visible. She took her time, moving with practiced ease, pausing occasionally to listen to the soft rustle of leaves and the distant call of birds. This part of Elaria was untouched by Ironhold's machines, but the whispers were still faint, as if even the deepest parts of the forest were holding their breath.

"This way," she murmured to herself, glancing at the twisted trunks that marked the start of the ancient trail. The bark of the trees here spiraled upwards, their trunks so thick that three grown men would struggle to wrap their arms around them. They were old sentinels, watching over paths forgotten by most—paths only known to those who took the time to listen.

"Twisted trunks," Lira whispered, running her fingers along the rough bark as she passed. "The trail starts here."

"Do you often talk to yourself, or is it just when you're lost?" a voice called from somewhere above her.

Lira stopped, looking up to see a young spirit sitting on one of the lower branches, legs swinging lazily. His form was small and agile, with hair that seemed to change color with the shifting light, and eyes that gleamed with mischief.

"Not lost," Lira replied, raising an eyebrow. "Just… finding my way."

"Finding?" the spirit echoed, a smirk playing on his lips. "Most who come here are either wandering aimlessly or running from something. Which one are you?"

"Neither," Lira said firmly, but with a hint of a smile. "I'm going to the Outer Grove. The older spirits are expecting me."

"Ah," the spirit replied, his smirk fading slightly. "The Outer Grove, is it? You must have quite the reason to visit *them*."

"I do," Lira said, looking back at the path ahead. "And it's important."

The spirit studied her for a moment, his gaze lingering on the determination in her eyes. "Well then," he said, hopping down gracefully from the branch and landing beside her, "you'd better be on your way. The Outer Grove doesn't wait for the uncertain."

"Thanks for the advice," Lira replied, giving him a nod before continuing along the path.

As she walked, she kept an eye out for the next landmark—the moonstone pillars. They were hidden within a shroud of mist, their surfaces slick with dew and almost invisible to the untrained eye. But Lira had learned to see what others missed. She reached the clearing, and there they were, two tall, slender stones that shimmered faintly in the haze.

"Moonstone pillars," Lira murmured, touching the cool surface of one of the stones. "Still standing after all these years."

She remembered Elder Ashen's stories about the pillars—how they were placed here by the first guardians of the forest, long before her time. They served as a silent reminder of the ancient pacts and the hidden paths that wound through Elaria like veins in a living body.

"Lira," another voice called out, this time from behind one of the pillars. A tall spirit emerged from the mist, her form shifting slightly, almost translucent in the moonlight. Her eyes were a pale silver, and her hair seemed to float as if caught in an unseen current.

"I didn't expect to see you here, Nissa," Lira greeted, recognizing the spirit immediately.

"Few come this way," Nissa replied, her voice like the soft rustling of leaves. "And even fewer know the paths as you do."

Lira smiled faintly. "I've walked these paths my whole life. The pillars haven't moved, even if everything else has."

Nissa tilted her head, watching Lira with a curious expression. "You seek the elders of the Outer Grove?"

"I do," Lira confirmed, adjusting the satchel slung over her shoulder. "There are questions I need answers to, and I believe they can help."

Nissa's eyes narrowed slightly, a hint of concern in her gaze. "The elders are wary of those who bring unrest. The balance here is delicate."

"I know," Lira said softly, looking back at the pillars. "But it's precisely because of that balance that I'm here. If Ironhold continues its advance, the balance won't just be delicate—it'll be broken."

Nissa remained silent for a moment, studying Lira as if weighing her sincerity. Finally, she nodded. "The path beyond the pillars will lead you to the Outer Grove," she said quietly. "But tread carefully. The spirits there are… not as forgiving as those you've met before."

"I understand," Lira replied, offering a small bow. "Thank you, Nissa."

"May the forest guide your steps," Nissa said, her form fading into the mist as she retreated back to her vigil by the pillars.

Lira continued forward, passing between the moonstone pillars and into a thicker part of the forest. The trees here grew closer together, their branches intertwining to create a natural archway overhead. The path was narrow and winding, with roots that jutted up from the ground like ancient fingers. Lira moved carefully, her steps sure and steady despite the rough terrain.

As she traveled, she couldn't help but think of the connections between these hidden places. Elder Ashen's grove, the Fae Court, the moonstone pillars, and now the Outer Grove—all were threads woven into the fabric of Elaria. She had walked these paths many times before, but now they felt different, as if the forest itself was urging her to see it with new eyes.

Eventually, she reached the edge of the Outer Grove. The air here was thick with the scent of earth and old wood, and the trees seemed to loom taller, their branches heavy with age and memory. Lira paused, taking a moment to steady her breathing before stepping into the clearing.

"You've come far, child of the forest," a deep voice greeted her.

Lira turned to see an elder spirit emerge from the shadows, his form massive and gnarled like the trunk of an ancient oak. His eyes were dark and piercing, and his presence radiated an unmistakable aura of authority.

"Elder Thorne," Lira greeted, bowing her head respectfully. "Thank you for allowing me into your grove."

"You walk paths that few remember," Thorne said, his voice like the creak of old wood. "Why have you come to the Outer Grove, Lira of Elaria?"

"I've come to seek your guidance," Lira replied, meeting his gaze steadily. "And to ask for your help in preserving the balance of Elaria."

The elder spirit watched her in silence, his eyes narrowing slightly as if assessing her words. Lira felt her heart quicken, the weight of the journey settling over her. She was in a place where time seemed to hold its breath, and she knew that what she said next would determine whether she was welcomed or turned away.

"I do not seek to disturb your peace," she continued, her voice steady despite her nerves. "But the forest is in danger, and I believe that only by understanding the old paths and the wisdom of the elders can we find a way to protect it."

Elder Thorne's eyes softened slightly, a hint of approval in his gaze. "You speak with humility and purpose," he said quietly. "Perhaps there is hope for you yet, child of the forest."

Lira let out a slow breath, feeling a sense of relief wash over her. The journey had been long, but she had made it. And now, in the heart of the Outer Grove, surrounded by the oldest spirits of Elaria, she felt a renewed sense of resolve.

The forest was not just a place—it was a living, breathing entity, and she was a part of it. And if she was to protect it, she would need to understand every path, every connection, and every voice that whispered through the leaves.

The forest darkened as Lira ventured deeper, its canopy thickening until only stray beams of sunlight pierced through the heavy branches. The path was narrow and winding, overgrown with ancient roots that seemed to curl around her feet like fingers trying to pull her down. Lira's footsteps were cautious but deliberate, her hand occasionally brushing against the trunks of the trees for balance and reassurance. She was searching for Old Moira, a spirit few dared to approach.

As she neared the heart of the secluded grove, the air seemed to change—cooler and tinged with a faint bitterness that prickled at her skin. Lira paused, steadying herself. She had heard tales of Old Moira's resentment, a bitterness rooted in memories of old betrayals and pain. Even the other spirits spoke of her in hushed tones, as if fearing that Moira's name alone could summon her wrath.

Lira took a deep breath and stepped into the clearing. There, standing tall and gnarled with age, was Moira. The old spirit was part of an immense, ancient tree whose trunk was marked with deep fissures that seemed to tell stories of their own. Moira's face, carved from the bark, was sharp and stern, her eyes like dark pools reflecting centuries of grief and anger.

"I was wondering when you would come," Moira's voice creaked, slow and heavy like old wood bending in a storm. She did not turn to face Lira, her eyes remaining fixed on the distant branches above. "The whispers warned me of a meddlesome child wandering into my grove."

Lira took another steadying breath. "I didn't mean to intrude," she said, her voice careful and respectful. "But I had to see you."

Moira let out a sound that was halfway between a sigh and a scoff. "They all say that," she replied, bitterness lacing her words. "The humans—they all come with apologies and empty promises. 'We didn't mean to intrude. We didn't mean to harm you.' But the forest remembers what your kind did."

"I know," Lira said softly, lowering her gaze. "I'm not here to ask for forgiveness for things I can't change. But I came because... because I need your help."

"Help?" Moira turned slightly, her ancient eyes narrowing as she finally looked at Lira. "Help with what, child?"

"Ironhold is spreading its influence," Lira began, choosing her words carefully. "They're capturing spirits, turning their pain into power for their machines. If they continue, the Breath of Elaria will weaken beyond saving."

Moira's eyes darkened, her branches creaking as if in pain. "You speak of the Breath of Elaria," she muttered, her voice thick with emotion. "The humans once spoke of it as a gift—a lifeblood to be cherished and protected. Now, they twist it to their own ends, and the forest suffers."

Lira took a step closer, her heart beating faster. "I don't want to be like them," she said, her voice trembling slightly. "I don't want to see the forest wither and the spirits suffer. I want to stop Ironhold, but I need guidance."

"Guidance?" Moira echoed, tilting her head slightly. "And why should I trust a human with such a request?"

"Because I'm not just human," Lira replied, her voice firm. "The forest chose me as its guardian. I can hear its whispers, feel its pain... and its hope."

Moira was silent for a long moment, studying Lira with an expression that was hard to read—caught somewhere between suspicion and curiosity. The wind picked up, rustling the leaves around them, and for a moment, it seemed as if the entire forest was holding its breath, waiting for Moira's response.

"Hope," Moira murmured, the word almost a sigh. She closed her eyes, her branches swaying slightly. "It has been a long time since I believed in hope."

Lira felt a pang of sympathy for the old spirit. She had known spirits who harbored bitterness towards humans, but Moira's pain seemed deeper, more personal. It wasn't just anger—it was grief, old and lingering, like a wound that refused to heal.

"I can't erase the past," Lira said softly, "but I can try to make things right. I can try to protect what remains."

Moira's eyes opened slowly, and she let out another creaking sigh. "You speak with conviction, child. Perhaps… perhaps there is more to you than the others."

Lira held her breath, waiting for Moira to continue.

"There are paths in this forest," Moira said quietly, her voice barely more than a whisper. "Paths that only the oldest spirits remember. Hidden tunnels that wind through the heart of the land, leading to places where even Ironhold's machines cannot tread."

"Hidden tunnels?" Lira echoed, leaning forward slightly. "Do you know where they lead?"

"To the places humans once feared," Moira replied, her eyes narrowing slightly. "Places where the ancient magics still linger. Ironhold's machines cannot reach these depths, but the passages are not easy to traverse. They are meant for spirits, not mortals."

"Can you show me these paths?" Lira asked, trying to keep the urgency from creeping into her voice.

Moira hesitated, her branches creaking as if in thought. "Why should I?" she asked, her tone sharp. "Why should I risk revealing the old ways to you?"

"Because if Ironhold succeeds," Lira said, meeting Moira's gaze, "there won't be any old ways left to protect."

The old spirit watched her in silence, her expression unreadable. Then, slowly, Moira nodded. "Very well," she said, her voice heavy with reluctant acceptance. "But know this, child of the forest—these paths are not without danger. The ancient magics that protect them are powerful and unpredictable."

"I understand," Lira replied, a note of determination in her voice. "I'm willing to take that risk."

Moira let out a weary sigh, her eyes closing for a moment. "You are braver than most," she muttered. "Or perhaps just more foolish. Time will tell."

Lira smiled faintly. "Maybe a little of both."

Moira's eyes opened once more, and for the first time, there was a glimmer of something other than bitterness in her gaze—something that might have been understanding. "Follow me," she said, turning towards the depths of the grove. "I will show you the old paths."

Lira followed silently, her heart pounding with a mixture of fear and hope. Moira's distrust hadn't vanished, but she had offered something far more valuable—guidance and a chance to change the course of things. And as Lira stepped deeper into the shadows of the grove, she felt her resolve harden.

There was still a long way to go, and many dangers yet to face, but at least now she wasn't walking the path alone.

Lira stood at the edge of the old moonstone circle, the ancient stones casting long shadows in the pale light. Her fingers traced the worn markings on one of the pillars, the engravings almost entirely faded by centuries of wind and rain. She took a deep breath, letting her eyes drift over the landscape before her—the sprawling forest of Elaria, filled with hidden paths, forgotten groves, and long-forgotten secrets.

"This land is more than just a forest," Lira murmured to herself, as if speaking would help her solidify her thoughts. "It's the lifeblood of every spirit that calls it home. And every path, every grove, holds a piece of its history."

"Talking to the stones again?" came a familiar voice.

Lira turned to see Nissa emerging from the shadows, her translucent form faintly shimmering in the dim light. Nissa's silver eyes held a mixture of curiosity and amusement as she approached.

"Not just the stones," Lira replied, smiling slightly. "The paths, the roots, the branches—they all have stories to tell."

"And you think those stories will help you bridge the gap between Ironhold and the Fae?" Nissa asked, her tone more questioning than accusatory.

"It's not just about the stories," Lira said, shaking her head. "It's about knowing the land—understanding how it connects us all. If I'm going to unite the spirits, the Fae, and even the humans willing to listen, I need to start with the land itself."

Nissa tilted her head, studying Lira with an almost childlike curiosity. "And you think that understanding this land will somehow… bring everyone together?"

Lira nodded. "Elaria is divided right now," she explained, her voice steady and thoughtful. "Not just by politics or mistrust, but physically. The Fae Court, Elder Ashen's Grove, the Outer Grove, Ironhold's Outskirts—each place is isolated. But if I can find the paths that connect them, I can bring people together in ways words alone can't."

Nissa raised an eyebrow, a hint of skepticism in her expression. "So, you think geography is the answer?"

"I think it's part of the answer," Lira replied, glancing back at the moonstone pillars. "The spirits have always told me that the land remembers more than we do. If I can understand it—if I can find the old paths and connect these places—I might be able to bring everyone to the same table."

Nissa let out a soft chuckle. "That's a lot of weight to put on the land."

"It's not just the land," Lira countered, her voice firm. "It's the people who live in it, the spirits who are part of it. They're all connected. It's like…" She paused, searching for the right metaphor. "It's like a web. Every thread matters, and if one is cut, the whole thing starts to unravel."

"And you're planning to be the weaver?" Nissa asked, her tone almost teasing.

Lira met her gaze steadily. "Someone has to be," she said, a quiet determination in her voice.

Nissa regarded her for a long moment, and then she sighed softly. "You're different, Lira," she said, her voice losing some of its playfulness. "Most who seek power or alliances only care about the ends. But you… you're looking at the means. At the paths that others overlook."

"Because those paths matter," Lira replied, almost as if reminding herself. "And if I can show people that—show them that the land can connect us instead of dividing us—it might be enough."

Nissa's eyes narrowed slightly, as if she were weighing Lira's words. Finally, she nodded. "There are old paths you haven't seen yet," she said quietly. "Paths that the Fae once walked, and tunnels beneath the ground that connect to the heart of Ironhold. If you can find those, it might be a start."

Lira's eyes widened slightly. "Do you know where they are?"

"I know where some of them are," Nissa replied, her voice barely above a whisper. "But finding them won't be easy. Some paths are hidden to mortal eyes—guarded by wards or shrouded in illusion."

"Can you help me find them?" Lira asked, her voice tinged with hope.

Nissa was silent for a moment, her eyes distant as if recalling a memory from long ago. "I can show you some of the old paths," she said finally. "But there are others that even I cannot reach. Paths that are known only to the oldest spirits."

"Then I'll find them," Lira said, her resolve hardening. "Even if it takes time, even if it's difficult. I'll find them."

Nissa shook her head, a faint smile on her lips. "You're stubborn," she remarked. "But maybe that's what the forest needs right now."

Lira smiled in return, feeling a flicker of warmth at Nissa's words. "Thank you," she said softly.

"Don't thank me yet," Nissa replied, her expression turning serious. "You're about to walk paths that haven't been traveled in centuries. And if you're not careful, you might not find your way back."

"I'll be careful," Lira promised. "And I'll listen to the forest. It hasn't led me astray yet."

Nissa nodded slowly. "Then follow me," she said, turning towards a narrow trail hidden between two ancient oaks. "This path will lead you to the old river crossing. From there, the land will guide you—if you're willing to listen."

Lira followed, her heart pounding with a mixture of anticipation and determination. As they walked, she mentally marked each turn, each landmark—a bent willow branch, a fallen birch tree with roots exposed, a moss-covered stone that seemed to glow faintly in the fading light. She knew that these markers would be crucial in the days to come, not just for herself, but for anyone who sought to travel these paths after her.

"Remember," Nissa said softly as they reached the edge of the river. "The old paths are not just physical—they're tied to the memories of the land. If you lose yourself, listen to the whispers, and they will guide you."

Lira nodded, her eyes scanning the riverbank. "I'll remember," she said quietly.

Nissa hesitated for a moment, as if wanting to say something more, but then she simply nodded. "Good luck, Lira of Elaria," she murmured, her voice almost lost in the rustle of the wind.

"Thank you, Nissa," Lira replied, watching as the spirit disappeared into the shadows of the forest. She turned back to the river, her eyes tracing its winding course as it flowed towards the horizon.

The path ahead was still uncertain, but as Lira marked the crossing in her mind, she felt a sense of clarity return. The land was more than just a place—it was a bridge between the past and the future, and between the people who called it home.

And if she was going to protect it, she needed to understand every twist, every turn, and every hidden thread that connected it all.

Chapter 8
A Warning Ignored

The path to the hidden grove was unlike any other in Elaria. Elder Ashen's roots extended deep into the earth, guiding Lira along a route that only he knew, twisting through dense underbrush and weaving between towering trees older than the songs whispered on the wind. The air was thick with anticipation, and even the forest seemed to hold its breath as they journeyed deeper into its ancient heart.

"You must listen carefully," Elder Ashen's voice resonated through the trees, the sound vibrating in Lira's chest like a distant drum. "The grove is not a place that welcomes strangers lightly."

"I'm not a stranger," Lira replied, her voice tinged with determination. "This forest is my home."

Elder Ashen's branches creaked in response, as if contemplating her words. "Home is more than a place," he murmured. "It is a bond—one that must be earned and honored."

Lira pressed on, feeling the ground beneath her soften with each step, the earth almost pliant under her feet. The further they went, the denser the trees became, their branches forming a canopy so thick that it blocked out the sun. What little light made it through painted the world in hues of deep green and shadowed gold.

As they moved deeper into the forest, Lira felt the air change. It became cooler, and the scent of old wood and damp earth filled her lungs. She could hear faint whispers around her, the murmur of ancient roots and the distant hum of something far more profound—a melody that seemed to come from everywhere and nowhere at once.

They reached the entrance to the hidden grove, a narrow gap between two immense trees whose roots intertwined in a tangled embrace. Elder Ashen's great branches swayed slightly, a gesture both of invitation and warning.

"Beyond this point lies the Song of the Trees," he said, his voice grave. "It is a song born of memory—of times of harmony, and times of betrayal. You must listen with your heart as much as your ears, Lira."

Lira took a deep breath, steeling herself for what lay ahead. She had come this far, and there was no turning back now. She stepped through the gap, feeling a rush of cold air wash over her, like stepping into a different world.

The grove was small and secluded, surrounded by trees that seemed to whisper in a language too old to fully comprehend. At the center stood an ancient oak, its trunk gnarled and twisted with age. A faint glow emanated from its roots, casting a soft light over the clearing. The air was alive with the hum of magic, and Lira felt it resonate deep within her bones.

Elder Ashen's voice drifted through the grove, softer now, almost like a lullaby. "Listen, Lira. Listen to the Song of the Trees."

Lira closed her eyes, allowing herself to focus on the sounds around her. At first, all she heard was the rustling of leaves and the creaking of branches. But then, slowly, the melody emerged—a haunting tune that seemed to rise from the roots of the ancient oak, carrying with it the weight of centuries.

It was a song of contrasts, of joy and sorrow interwoven like threads in a tapestry. Lira could hear the echoes of laughter, the soft murmur of voices speaking in harmony with the forest. But those moments were fleeting, swallowed by a deeper, more resonant sound—one of pain and loss, of anger and betrayal.

She felt the memories in the melody, as if the forest itself were sharing its secrets with her. She saw visions of the past, fleeting images that flickered like shadows in her mind. She saw the spirits, once vibrant and free, moving through the trees with grace and purpose. She saw humans and spirits working side by side, cultivating the land in harmony.

But then, the melody shifted, and the harmony gave way to discord. Lira saw the faces of humans twisted with ambition, their eyes filled with hunger for power. She heard the clash of iron against wood, the cries of spirits as they were captured and bound. The betrayal was palpable, a scar etched into the very heart of Elaria.

The melody reached a crescendo, and Lira felt the weight of it pressing down on her, the pain and anger overwhelming her senses. It was as if the forest were trying to communicate something to her—something ancient and powerful, a warning and a plea all at once.

She stumbled, her knees buckling beneath the weight of the song. She could feel the magic thrumming through the air, growing stronger and more intense with each passing moment. It was as if the grove itself were alive, the trees breathing in time with the melody.

"Elder Ashen," she gasped, her voice trembling. "What... what is this?"

"This is the heart of Elaria," the ancient tree replied, his voice a deep rumble. "The memory of what was, and the echo of what still lingers."

"It's... too much," Lira whispered, her hands trembling as she reached out to steady herself against the ancient oak. The melody seemed to pulse through her, a living thing that resonated with her very soul. She felt as if she were being pulled apart, the memories of the forest intermingling with her own thoughts and emotions.

"You must hold on, Guardian," Elder Ashen urged, his tone both firm and gentle. "The Song is not meant to break you, but to guide you."

Lira closed her eyes, trying to focus on her breathing, on the connection she shared with the forest. She could feel the memories pulling at her, threatening to drown her in their depths. But she couldn't let that happen. She had to find a way to anchor herself, to separate her own thoughts from the pain of the past.

Slowly, she took a deep breath, grounding herself in the present. She focused on the rhythm of the melody, allowing it to flow through her without losing herself to it. The pain was still there, but she could feel a deeper understanding taking root—an awareness of the forest's history, of its wounds and its strength.

As the melody began to fade, Lira opened her eyes, her breathing still uneven. She felt drained, as if the Song had taken something from her, but it had also given her something in return—a glimpse into the soul of Elaria.

"The Song," Lira murmured, her voice barely a whisper. "It's… powerful."

"It is the voice of the forest," Elder Ashen replied, his tone solemn. "A voice that carries the weight of memory and the promise of what could be."

Lira looked up at the ancient oak, a sense of awe mingling with the lingering pain. She understood now why the grove was hidden, why the Song was not meant for all ears. It was both a gift and a burden, a reminder of the delicate balance that held Elaria together.

And within the Song, she felt the shadow of something else—something vast and ancient, a power that, if unleashed, could reshape the world.

"Elder," Lira said softly, her voice tinged with both reverence and fear, "what… what will happen if this power is unleashed?"

"That," Elder Ashen replied, his voice echoing like distant thunder, "is a question only you can answer, Guardian of Elaria."

Lira swallowed hard, feeling the weight of his words settle over her like a heavy cloak. The path ahead was fraught with danger and uncertainty, but she knew now that the forest held more secrets than she had ever imagined—and more power than she had ever dared to hope for.

Lira remained in the hidden grove, her breathing steadying as she tried to process the intensity of the Song. The grove seemed to pulse with life, the trees' roots weaving a tapestry of old memories beneath her feet. The whispers of the past still lingered in the air, like echoes in a vast, empty hall. She could feel the weight of the forest's history pressing down on her, as if it were waiting for something—an answer, a decision, a choice.

Elder Ashen's presence filled the grove, his ancient branches stretching out like arms reaching towards the sky. The great oak's voice resonated through the clearing, a low rumble that seemed to carry the weight of centuries. "Lira," he murmured, his tone both solemn and cautious, "you have heard the Song of the Trees, but there is more you must understand."

Lira took a deep breath, steadying herself. "I'm listening," she replied, her voice still shaky but firm.

Elder Ashen's branches rustled softly, as if he were gathering his thoughts. "The Song you heard is not merely a memory," he said slowly. "It is the lifeblood of the forest, the essence of what was and what could be. It carries within it the power to heal, but also the power to destroy."

Lira frowned, a chill running down her spine. "Destroy?" she echoed, her voice tinged with confusion. "But… it felt like the forest was trying to show me something—something important."

The old tree spirit sighed, the sound like a gust of wind rustling through dry leaves. "It was," he admitted. "The Song is a gift, Lira, but it is also a great burden. To invoke it is to call upon the deepest roots of Elaria's magic—the magic of creation and decay, of life and death."

Lira's fingers tightened around the edge of her cloak, her thoughts racing. She had felt the power in the Song, but she hadn't understood its full implications. "You're saying… if I invoke the Song, I could harm the forest?" she asked, trying to keep her voice steady.

Elder Ashen's branches creaked, his leaves swaying gently in the cool breeze. "If the Song is invoked without understanding, it could unbalance the very heart of Elaria," he warned. "The spirits bound within the Song are ancient, their pain and anger woven into its melody. If that anger is released unchecked, it could spread like wildfire, consuming everything in its path."

Lira felt a cold knot form in her stomach. She had thought the Song was the key to restoring balance, to mending the wounds left by Ironhold's greed and ambition. But now, she realized that it was far more dangerous than she had imagined.

"What should I do, then?" she asked quietly, her voice almost a whisper. "If invoking the Song could destroy everything, how can I use it to save the forest?"

The great oak was silent for a long moment, the weight of the question hanging heavily between them. When Elder Ashen finally spoke, his voice was softer, almost sorrowful. "That is a choice only you can make, Guardian," he said. "The Song is a double-edged blade—capable of cutting away the darkness, but also capable of cutting into the heart of what it seeks to protect."

Lira closed her eyes, her mind racing. She had come to the grove seeking answers, but all she had found were more questions. She could still hear the Song faintly in the back of her mind, its melody beckoning to her, promising salvation but whispering of ruin.

"If I do nothing," she said, her voice barely audible, "Ironhold will continue to capture and corrupt the spirits. The forest will keep suffering."

"Yes," Elder Ashen agreed, his voice heavy with regret. "And if you invoke the Song, there is a chance you could stop Ironhold's advance—banish the corruption and heal the wounds that have been inflicted upon Elaria."

"But there's also a chance I could destroy everything," Lira murmured, her voice trembling slightly.

Elder Ashen's branches swayed, the sound like a mournful sigh. "The Song is not meant to be a weapon, Lira," he said gently. "It is a reminder of what was lost, and a plea for what could be. If you invoke it with anger or fear in your heart, it could amplify those emotions and turn them into something terrible."

Lira felt a shiver run through her, the realization of what Elder Ashen was saying sinking in. "Then… how do I know if I'm ready?" she asked, her voice laced with doubt.

"You must listen to the forest," Elder Ashen replied. "Truly listen. The Song is not yours to control, nor is it something you can wield without consequence. It is a bond between you and Elaria—a bond that must be earned and respected."

Lira took a deep breath, trying to steady her racing thoughts. She felt the weight of the decision pressing down on her, the enormity of what lay ahead almost suffocating. She had never imagined that her role as a guardian would demand such a choice—a choice that could either save the forest or doom it to another cycle of destruction.

"What if I make the wrong choice?" she asked softly, her voice almost breaking.

Elder Ashen's leaves rustled gently, his voice warm and reassuring. "We all fear making the wrong choice," he said. "But it is not the choice itself that defines us—it is the intention behind it. If you act with a pure heart, with the desire to protect and heal, the Song will guide you."

Lira nodded slowly, trying to absorb his words. She had spent so long fighting to protect the forest, to defend the spirits and the balance that held Elaria together. But this... this was different. It wasn't just about fighting—it was about understanding, about listening to the ancient magic that flowed through the roots and branches of the forest.

"I'll try," she said quietly, her voice filled with determination. "I'll listen."

Elder Ashen's branches creaked softly, his tone gentle and encouraging. "That is all we can do, Guardian—try and listen."

Lira took one last look at the ancient grove, the memory of the Song still lingering in the air like a distant melody. She didn't have all the answers, and the path ahead was fraught with danger and uncertainty. But she knew now that she couldn't turn away from this burden, no matter how heavy it was.

"Thank you, Elder," she murmured, her voice sincere.

"May the forest guide you, Lira," Elder Ashen replied, his voice carrying the weight of both hope and caution. "And may you find the strength to carry this burden without letting it consume you."

As Lira left the grove, the whispers of the ancient trees seemed to follow her, their voices a quiet reminder of the choice she would one day have to make. It was a choice that could either save Elaria or doom it to another cycle of pain and betrayal.

And deep down, she knew that whatever path she chose, it would change the fate of the forest—and her own fate—forever.

The journey back from the hidden grove was a silent one. The forest was alive with its usual sounds—the rustle of leaves in the wind, the occasional call of a night bird—but to Lira, it felt as if the world had become muted, every noise softened under the weight of the thoughts racing through her mind. She replayed Elder Ashen's warning over and over, his words like a heavy stone sinking deeper into her chest.

The Song is not meant to be a weapon… It is a bond that must be earned and respected.

She stopped at the edge of a small clearing where the moonlight poured in, painting the grass in silver. It was a place she often came to think, a place where the canopy of trees parted just enough to allow the night sky to peek through. Lira's heart was heavy with the knowledge she had gained, with the realization that the responsibility of invoking the Song carried far greater risks than she had anticipated.

"I don't know if I'm strong enough," she murmured to herself, the words barely louder than a breath.

"You question yourself often," a familiar voice replied.

Lira turned to see Farael stepping from the shadows, his form almost blending with the night mist. His luminous eyes reflected the moonlight, studying her intently. There was a familiarity in his presence, an anchor that kept her from completely losing herself in the sea of doubt.

"I'm the Guardian of this forest," Lira replied, trying to steady her voice. "If I can't protect it, then what good am I?"

"You are not just a title, Lira," Farael countered, his voice gentle but firm. "You are more than the sum of your duties."

Lira let out a bitter laugh, her shoulders slumping slightly. "It doesn't feel like it," she admitted. "Every decision I make feels like it's leading us closer to disaster."

Farael remained silent for a moment, his gaze unwavering. "Doubt is not a sign of weakness," he said softly. "It is a sign that you understand the gravity of your choices. The reckless do not question themselves—only the wise do."

Lira turned away, looking up at the sky. "Elder Ashen said the Song could destroy the forest if I'm not careful," she said, her voice carrying a faint tremor. "What if I lose control? What if, in trying to save Elaria, I end up destroying everything?"

Farael stepped closer, his voice a quiet murmur in the darkness. "The Song of the Trees is not just a power to wield," he said. "It is a reflection of the heart of Elaria—and of your own heart as well. It will respond to what lies within you, Lira. That is why you must be certain of your intentions, and of the burden you are willing to bear."

Lira clenched her fists, frustration and fear warring within her. "How can I be certain when everything feels so uncertain?" she demanded, her voice breaking. "How can I be sure that I'm doing the right thing?"

Farael was silent for a long moment, the wind rustling through his mist-like fur. When he finally spoke, his voice was softer than she had ever heard it. "You cannot be certain," he admitted. "No one can. But that does not mean you are without a guide."

"What guide?" Lira asked, her voice laced with skepticism. "The spirits? The forest? They're all looking to me for answers."

"Your heart," Farael replied, his gaze piercing. "The part of you that has always sought to protect, even when the path was unclear. The part of you that reached out to those who would not trust you, because you believed it was the right thing to do. That is your guide, Lira."

Lira's anger and frustration seemed to ebb, replaced by a quiet understanding. She took a deep breath, trying to center herself amidst the turmoil within. Farael's words struck a chord in her—an echo of the promises she had made to the spirits, to the forest, and to herself.

"I made a vow," she said softly, almost to herself. "To protect this forest, no matter the cost."

Farael nodded, his form seeming to blur slightly in the dim light. "And that vow has carried you this far. It is not wrong to fear losing yourself, Lira. But remember, the forest chose you not because you are perfect, but because you are willing to face that fear."

Lira felt a warmth spread through her chest, a flicker of hope that pushed back the shadows of doubt. She looked up at the ancient trees around her, their branches swaying gently in the night breeze. She could still feel the presence of the Song, a distant melody waiting for her to decide whether or not to embrace it.

"Maybe I'm not strong enough," she murmured, her voice steadying. "But if I don't try, then what's the point of being the Guardian?"

Farael inclined his head slightly, his eyes reflecting the moonlight like twin stars. "Strength is not the absence of fear, Lira," he said quietly. "It is the courage to keep going despite it."

Lira closed her eyes, taking a slow breath as she let Farael's words sink in. She couldn't let fear dictate her choices, not when so much was at stake. The Song was a powerful force, one that could either heal or destroy. And if she was going to use it, she needed to be prepared to accept whatever consequences came with that choice.

She opened her eyes, her resolve growing stronger. "I'll find a way to use the Song without destroying Elaria," she said, her voice carrying a quiet determination. "Even if it means losing a part of myself in the process."

Farael's expression softened, a rare flicker of pride in his eyes. "You have always carried the forest within you," he said. "And no matter what path you choose, that will not change."

Lira felt a sense of clarity settle over her, the fear and doubt still present but no longer overwhelming. She knew the risks, and she knew that the path ahead was fraught with uncertainty. But she also knew that she couldn't turn away from this responsibility—not when so many lives depended on her.

"I won't let the Song become a weapon," she vowed quietly, her voice barely more than a whisper. "I'll use it to protect what's left… and to honor what was lost."

Farael inclined his head, a gesture of both acknowledgment and respect. "The forest chose well," he said softly. "You are more than a Guardian, Lira. You are a protector of hope."

As Lira stood there in the moonlit clearing, the weight of her duty seemed to settle over her like a cloak—not a burden, but a mantle that she had chosen to wear. She still didn't have all the answers, and the fear of failure lingered in the back of her mind. But she was no longer paralyzed by it.

She turned to Farael, her gaze steady. "Thank you," she said sincerely.

"Thank me by continuing to listen to your heart," Farael replied, his form slowly dissipating into the night mist. "And by trusting in yourself, even when the path is unclear."

Lira watched as the mist-wolf faded into the shadows, leaving her alone in the moonlit clearing. The forest around her seemed to hum with life, the trees swaying gently as if acknowledging her resolve.

She took a deep breath, feeling the steady rhythm of the forest's heartbeat resonate within her. And as she stood there, listening to the whispers of the ancient trees, she felt a quiet determination take root—a resolve to find a way forward, no matter how difficult it might be.

Lira was the Guardian of Elaria, and she would not let the Song become a harbinger of destruction. Not while she still had the strength to protect those she held dear.

Chapter 9
Desperation and Resolve

The grand halls of Ironhold's central tower were eerily quiet at night. The thick stone walls seemed to absorb every whisper, every footstep, leaving only the low hum of machinery to break the silence. Fenn walked quickly, keeping his head down as he made his way through the dimly lit corridors. He didn't want to be here—he didn't want to overhear what he knew he shouldn't—but something inside him compelled him to seek the truth.

He reached the archway leading to the Chancellor's private study, a room reserved for secretive councils and decisions that never made it to the city's public forums. Fenn pressed his back against the cold stone wall, straining to hear the voices inside. The Chancellor's deep, authoritative tone was unmistakable, carrying through the closed door like the distant roll of thunder.

"The new sacrifices will be chosen from among the lower districts," the Chancellor was saying, his voice cold and devoid of hesitation. "The outer sectors are full of those who contribute little to Ironhold's progress. It's a necessary purge for the greater good."

Fenn's breath caught in his throat. He leaned closer, his heart pounding in his chest.

"Is it wise to deplete our workforce, Chancellor?" another voice asked—calm, measured, and filled with a quiet concern. It was Master Alchemist Yara, one of the Chancellor's most trusted advisors. "If word spreads, there could be unrest. Even rebellion."

The Chancellor's tone hardened. "Unrest is a risk we must be willing to take. Ironhold's future depends on the continued supply of spirit energy. Our success—our survival—requires sacrifice."

Fenn's hands clenched into fists. He had suspected Ironhold's leadership of corruption, but hearing the plan laid out so callously made his blood run cold. This wasn't just about controlling the forest or fighting off perceived threats. The Chancellor was willing to sacrifice their own people, feeding them to the spirit engines as fuel for his twisted vision of progress.

He couldn't listen to any more. The truth was a weight that pressed down on him, suffocating and cold. Fenn turned and hurried away, his mind racing. He needed to warn someone, to stop this madness before it went any further. But as he rounded the corner, he nearly collided with Brayden, who stood waiting with arms crossed, a stern expression on his face.

"Fenn," Brayden said, his voice clipped and full of suspicion. "What are you doing skulking around at this hour?"

Fenn's pulse quickened, and he forced a tight smile, trying to mask his fear. "Just… working late," he said, his voice faltering slightly.

Brayden's eyes narrowed, and he took a step closer, his presence looming. "Is that so?" he asked, his tone cold.

"Because from where I was standing, it looked like you were eavesdropping on the Chancellor's private meeting."

"I—" Fenn stammered, but Brayden cut him off.

"Don't lie to me," Brayden snapped, his eyes hardening. "You think I haven't noticed your recent… behavior? The questions, the hesitation, the time you spend away from the workshops. You're up to something, Fenn."

Fenn swallowed hard, trying to find the words to defuse the situation. But the look in Brayden's eyes told him it was too late for that.

"What did you hear?" Brayden demanded, his voice dropping to a dangerous whisper.

"Enough," Fenn replied, his voice trembling with barely-contained anger. "Enough to know that the Chancellor is planning to sacrifice innocent people to power his machines. Our own citizens, Brayden! This isn't progress—it's murder!"

Brayden's expression darkened, and he took another step forward, his voice low and menacing. "You're letting your emotions cloud your judgment," he said, his tone dripping with disdain. "You're starting to sound like the traitors and dissenters who want to see Ironhold fall."

"Traitors?" Fenn repeated, incredulity and fury mingling in his voice. "They're trying to stop this madness! Don't you see what's happening, Brayden? The Chancellor isn't saving Ironhold—he's destroying it from within!"

Brayden's jaw tightened, and he shook his head slowly, disappointment etched into his features. "I always knew you were weak, Fenn," he said, his voice laced with bitterness. "But I never thought you'd betray everything we've worked for."

"Betray?" Fenn's voice rose, his fists shaking with rage. "Brayden, I'm trying to save people—our people! The Chancellor's plan will destroy us all!"

Brayden's eyes flashed with anger, and he grabbed Fenn by the front of his coat, pulling him close. "Listen to me," he hissed. "The Chancellor is doing what needs to be done. If a few lives have to be sacrificed for the greater good, then so be it. That's the price of progress."

Fenn struggled against Brayden's grip, his voice trembling with desperation. "This isn't progress," he said, his eyes pleading with his friend to understand. "It's cruelty—it's madness!"

Brayden released him, shoving him back with a sneer. "You've lost your way," he said coldly. "You've been spending too much time listening to those forest dwellers and their lies. You're blinded by their false promises of peace and harmony."

Fenn staggered but quickly regained his footing, his heart pounding with fear and determination. "And you're blinded by loyalty to a man who's willing to sacrifice you just as easily as anyone else," he retorted. "Can't you see that, Brayden? You're just a pawn in his game."

Brayden's fists clenched, and for a moment, Fenn thought he might strike him. But instead, Brayden's expression hardened into something colder, something final. "If you go down this path, Fenn," he said quietly, his voice filled with an eerie calm, "then you're not just turning your back on the Chancellor—you're turning your back on me."

Fenn felt his chest tighten, the weight of the choice bearing down on him. Brayden had been his friend for years, a constant in the ever-changing world of Ironhold. But the man standing before him now was a stranger, loyal to a cause that Fenn could no longer support.

"I can't follow the Chancellor's orders, Brayden," Fenn said, his voice breaking slightly. "Not when they lead to this kind of horror."

Brayden stared at him, a mixture of anger and hurt flashing across his face. "Then you're a traitor," he said, his voice full of cold finality. "And you're no friend of mine."

Fenn opened his mouth to respond, but no words came. The reality of what had just happened settled over him like a heavy shroud—he had lost Brayden, and he had crossed a line that there was no going back from.

Without another word, Brayden turned and walked away, his footsteps echoing through the empty corridor. Fenn stood there, his heart aching with the weight of his decision and the knowledge of what was to come.

He couldn't stay in Ironhold any longer. Not after what he had learned. And as much as it hurt to lose Brayden's friendship, he knew he couldn't turn back now.

Fenn took a deep breath, his resolve hardening. He had to warn Lira, to stop the Chancellor's plan before more innocent lives were lost. Even if it meant betraying everything he had once believed in, even if it meant becoming an enemy of the city he once called home.

There was no turning back now.

Fenn paced through the dimly lit corridors of Ironhold's central tower, the Chancellor's words echoing relentlessly in his mind. Each step he took seemed to bring him closer to an inevitable confrontation with a truth he could no longer deny. The weight of what he had overheard settled heavily on his shoulders, and he felt the walls closing in, the dark stone halls now seeming more like a prison than a fortress.

He reached the central courtyard, where moonlight spilled through high windows, casting long shadows across the marble floor. Fenn paused, his breath shallow, as he saw Brayden standing there, waiting. The tension in the air was palpable, charged with the unspoken conflict that had been brewing between them.

"Brayden," Fenn called, his voice breaking the heavy silence. He tried to keep his tone steady, but the strain was evident. "We need to talk."

Brayden turned, his eyes narrowing. "We've talked enough," he replied coldly, his hands clenched at his sides. "I know where you've been, Fenn. And I know what you're planning."

Fenn swallowed, forcing himself to meet his friend's gaze. "You don't understand," he said, trying to keep his voice calm. "I overheard the Chancellor's plan. He's going to sacrifice more people—innocent people—to fuel the machines. We can't let this happen."

Brayden's expression hardened, and he took a step closer, his jaw clenched. "You're letting your emotions cloud your judgment," he snapped, his voice laced with frustration. "The Chancellor is doing what needs to be done. You knew the cost of progress when you signed up for this."

"I didn't sign up to watch our own people get sacrificed like livestock!" Fenn retorted, anger flaring in his voice. "This isn't progress, Brayden—it's murder."

Brayden's eyes flashed with anger, and he closed the distance between them, his voice dropping to a dangerous whisper. "You're talking like one of those forest rebels," he said. "You're letting their lies get into your head."

"It's not lies," Fenn shot back, his voice trembling with conviction. "I've seen the spirits trapped in those machines. I've heard their cries, their pain. And now I find out that the Chancellor is willing to sacrifice anyone—anyone—to keep those machines running? How can you stand by and support that?"

"Because it's necessary!" Brayden shouted, his voice echoing through the empty hall. He took a deep breath, trying to regain his composure. When he spoke again, his voice was lower, but no less intense. "Ironhold needs those machines to survive. Without them, the city will fall. People will die anyway. The Chancellor is doing what he must to protect our future."

Fenn shook his head, his eyes filled with disbelief. "You really believe that, don't you?" he said softly. "You believe that sacrificing innocent lives is worth it, as long as it keeps the city running."

Brayden's expression twisted with a mixture of anger and sadness. "I believe in Ironhold," he said firmly. "And I believe in the Chancellor's vision. He's the only one who understands what needs to be done to keep our city strong."

"Strong?" Fenn repeated, his voice rising in frustration. "This isn't strength, Brayden—it's cruelty. It's blind loyalty to a man who's leading us down a path of destruction."

"Blind loyalty?" Brayden's voice was bitter, his eyes narrowing. "You're the one who's been led astray, Fenn. You've been spending too much time out there in that forest, listening to their lies and forgetting where you belong."

"I haven't forgotten where I belong," Fenn said, his voice trembling with emotion. "But I can't ignore what I've seen, what I know. And I can't stand by and let this continue, Brayden. Not when I have a chance to stop it."

Brayden's face hardened, and he shook his head slowly. "You're making a mistake," he warned, his voice cold and distant. "If you go against the Chancellor, you're not just betraying Ironhold—you're betraying everything we've worked for."

Fenn felt a pang of guilt and sorrow, the weight of Brayden's words pressing down on him like a leaden shroud. But he knew he couldn't turn back now. He couldn't let fear or loyalty keep him from doing what was right.

"I'm trying to save lives," Fenn said quietly, his voice filled with conviction. "I'm trying to stop more people from suffering."

Brayden's eyes narrowed, his fists clenching at his sides. "You think you're the hero in this story," he said, his voice dripping with bitterness. "But all you're doing is tearing everything apart."

Fenn shook his head, his voice steady despite the turmoil inside him. "If protecting innocent lives means tearing apart a system built on suffering," he said firmly, "then so be it."

Brayden stared at him, his expression one of betrayal and hurt. For a moment, Fenn saw a flicker of something else—doubt, perhaps, or regret. But it was gone as quickly as it appeared, replaced by a steely resolve.

"If you go through with this," Brayden said slowly, his voice barely above a whisper, "then you're not just my enemy—you're the enemy of Ironhold."

Fenn felt a sharp pain in his chest, a deep sadness that threatened to overwhelm him. He had always considered Brayden more than just a friend—he had been like a brother.

But now, they were standing on opposite sides of a chasm that seemed impossible to bridge.

"I don't want to fight you, Brayden," Fenn said softly, his voice filled with a quiet plea. "But I can't let this continue."

Brayden's expression hardened, and he took a step back, his eyes filled with a cold determination. "Then you leave me no choice," he said, his voice trembling with barely-contained anger. "If you try to stop the Chancellor's plan, I will stop you. And I won't hold back."

Fenn felt a lump form in his throat, but he forced himself to nod. "Then do what you have to do," he replied, his voice heavy with sadness. "But I won't let more people die for the Chancellor's ambitions."

Brayden's eyes were hard, and for a moment, it seemed like he might lash out. But instead, he turned sharply and walked away, his footsteps echoing through the corridor like the toll of a funeral bell.

Fenn stood there, his heart aching with the weight of the confrontation. He had lost his closest friend, and he knew there was no going back now. The line had been drawn, and they were on opposite sides.

As the silence settled around him, Fenn felt a quiet resolve hardening within him. He couldn't save Brayden from his loyalty to Ironhold, but he could still try to save the people who were being sacrificed in the name of progress.

He took a deep breath, steeling himself for what lay ahead. The road was uncertain, and the price of his choices would be high. But he knew that doing nothing was no longer an option.

Fenn turned and walked away from the courtyard, the memory of Brayden's words echoing in his mind like a warning and a challenge all at once.

The air in the heart of the forest felt heavy with tension as Lira approached the clearing where Kara waited. The moonlight filtering through the thick canopy cast dappled shadows on the ancient stones that encircled the glade. The Fae leader stood at the center, her posture rigid, her silver hair catching the light like a blade. Her eyes, sharp and cautious, followed Lira's every move.

Lira stopped a few paces away, keeping her movements deliberate. She knew that any sign of weakness or hesitation would be met with disdain—or worse, dismissal. The Fae had little patience for what they saw as human frailty, and Kara, their leader, was no exception.

"Kara," Lira greeted, trying to keep her voice steady. "Thank you for meeting with me."

Kara's eyes narrowed, and she inclined her head slightly, a gesture that felt more like a warning than an acknowledgment. "You've been persistent," she said, her tone clipped. "And reckless. You're risking the safety of the forest with your constant meddling."

Lira took a deep breath, choosing her words carefully. "I'm trying to protect the forest," she replied. "Just as you are."

The Fae leader tilted her head, her expression unreadable. "And yet you seek alliances with those who would see us broken," she said, her voice edged with bitterness. "Humans, spirits, even the Wild Ones—creatures who owe no loyalty to the Fae. Do you believe that will be enough to stop Ironhold?"

"I believe that we can't afford to be divided," Lira said firmly. "Ironhold's machines are advancing, and every moment we spend arguing among ourselves is a moment lost. If we don't stand together, we'll all fall."

Kara's lips pressed into a thin line, her gaze never leaving Lira's face. "You speak of unity as if it's something easily achieved," she said quietly. "But you forget that there are wounds between us that have never healed. Trust cannot be forged with words alone, Guardian."

"I know," Lira admitted, her voice softening. "And I don't expect you to trust me—not completely. But I'm not asking for blind faith. I'm asking for a chance to prove that we can do this, together."

There was a long silence, the only sound the faint rustling of leaves in the breeze. Lira felt the weight of Kara's scrutiny, the unspoken judgment in her gaze. She knew that the Fae leader had every reason to refuse, every reason to turn her away. But she also knew that if Kara walked away now, the battle would be lost before it even began.

Kara let out a slow breath, her eyes narrowing. "You're asking for a truce," she said, her tone laced with reluctance.

"Yes," Lira replied. "A truce, for the sake of Elaria."

The Fae leader studied her for a moment longer, and Lira could see the internal struggle playing out behind her eyes. Kara was a warrior, a protector of her people, and her mistrust of humans ran deep. But there was something else there, too—a flicker of understanding, or perhaps recognition of the desperation they both shared.

"Very well," Kara said finally, her voice heavy with resignation. "I will join you, Guardian. But understand this—this alliance is born of necessity, not trust. If you betray the forest, or my people, I will not hesitate to act."

Lira felt a wave of relief wash over her, though she kept her expression steady. "I understand," she replied, her voice steady despite the weight of Kara's warning. "And I promise, I won't betray you."

Kara's eyes narrowed slightly, as if testing the sincerity in Lira's voice. "We shall see," she murmured, her tone carrying a hint of caution. "But know this—if you falter, if you let your emotions or your human ties cloud your judgment, I will end this truce."

Lira met her gaze, the intensity of the moment settling over them like a shroud. "I won't falter," she said firmly. "Not when so much is at stake."

The Fae leader was silent for a long moment, her eyes searching Lira's face for any sign of weakness or deceit. Finally, she nodded once, a curt, almost reluctant acknowledgment.

"Then we have an understanding," Kara said quietly.

Lira let out a slow breath, feeling the tension in her shoulders ease slightly. It wasn't trust, not yet, but it was a start. An uneasy truce, born of desperation and necessity, but essential nonetheless.

"I won't waste this chance," Lira said softly, her voice carrying both gratitude and determination. "Thank you."

Kara's expression didn't soften, but there was a glimmer of something else in her eyes—perhaps a hint of respect, or at the very least, acknowledgment of the risk Lira had taken by reaching out. "Do not thank me yet," she replied. "This alliance is as fragile as the branches of the young saplings. It will take more than promises to strengthen it."

"I know," Lira said. "And I'll do whatever it takes to prove that this was the right choice."

Kara inclined her head slightly, her silver hair shimmering in the moonlight. "I hope, for all our sakes, that you are right," she said. "But remember, Guardian—if you lead us astray, I will be the first to bring you to account."

With those parting words, Kara turned and walked away, her steps silent on the soft forest floor. Lira watched her go, feeling a mixture of relief and apprehension. The truce was a fragile thing, built on a foundation of necessity and desperation, but it was more than she had dared to hope for.

As the moonlight filtered through the leaves above, Lira felt a quiet resolve take root within her. Kara's warning echoed in her mind, a reminder of the fragility of their alliance and the weight of the responsibility she carried. But it also fueled her determination—a determination to prove that unity was possible, that this fragile bond could be strengthened and made whole.

"Thank you," Lira whispered to the silent trees around her, her voice carrying a promise to the forest she had sworn to protect. "I won't let you down."

The forest seemed to breathe in response, the ancient trees swaying gently in the breeze as if acknowledging her words. Lira stood there for a moment longer, feeling the gravity of the choices she had made and the path that lay ahead.

An alliance had been forged, however uneasy, and now it was up to her to see it through. For Elaria, for the spirits, and for those who still believed in the hope of a united forest.

Chapter 10
Breaking Point

Fenn leaned over the engine schematic, his eyes narrowing as he reviewed the latest modifications. The workshop was dimly lit, the only sources of light being the flickering lanterns hanging from the rafters and the soft glow of the engine's core on the workbench. It was late, long past the time when most engineers would have retired for the night, but Fenn couldn't bring himself to leave. Not with the questions gnawing at him.

He adjusted his glasses and focused on the containment runes etched into the engine's core. They were more intricate than any runes he had worked with before—delicate lines that seemed to pulse faintly with a reddish light. Fenn frowned, his hand hovering over the schematic, fingers twitching slightly as if he were hesitant to even touch it.

"It shouldn't be doing that," he muttered to himself, his voice barely above a whisper.

"What shouldn't be doing what?" came Brayden's voice from behind him, startling Fenn out of his thoughts.

Fenn turned quickly, his heartbeat quickening. "Brayden," he said, forcing a smile. "I didn't hear you come in."

Brayden leaned against the doorway, a smirk playing at the corner of his lips. "I figured you'd still be here, burning the midnight oil," he replied. "You know, they say it's not good to work yourself into the ground."

"I just… couldn't sleep," Fenn admitted, trying to keep his voice steady. "There's something off about these new runes."

Brayden raised an eyebrow. "Off how?" he asked, stepping closer to peer over Fenn's shoulder.

Fenn hesitated, glancing back at the runes. "They're reactive," he said slowly. "More than they should be. The energy in the core—it feels like it's… resisting."

"Resisting?" Brayden echoed, his tone skeptical. "Fenn, it's just energy. It's not alive."

"I know," Fenn said quickly. "But it's not just about the energy. The spirits that power these cores—they're not like the old ones. They're… different."

Brayden chuckled, patting Fenn on the back. "You've been spending too much time in here, my friend," he said lightly. "You're starting to sound like one of those old legends—'the spirits are alive, they have feelings,' all that nonsense."

"It's not nonsense," Fenn insisted, his voice firmer than he intended. "I've seen it, Brayden. The way the cores react when the spirits are captured—the runes flare up, almost like they're in pain."

Brayden's smile faded slightly, and he studied Fenn with a more serious expression. "Fenn," he said quietly, "you know better than anyone that these machines are our future. The Chancellor's made it clear that this is the only way forward."

"But at what cost?" Fenn asked, his voice barely more than a whisper.

There was a long silence, and Brayden let out a sigh. "Look," he said, his tone softening, "I get that you have reservations. But these spirits—they're just resources. The Chancellor wouldn't do anything to harm them if it wasn't absolutely necessary."

"Wouldn't he?" Fenn replied, his eyes narrowing. "You've seen the new containment protocols. They're designed to suppress any... resistance. Why would we need those if this was all as safe as he claims?"

Brayden hesitated, his expression wavering. "The Chancellor is a cautious man," he said, but there was less conviction in his voice now. "He's just taking precautions."

"Precautions?" Fenn echoed, bitterness creeping into his voice. "Or is he hiding something from us?"

Brayden sighed again, rubbing the back of his neck. "Fenn," he said quietly, "sometimes, you just have to trust that the people in charge know what they're doing."

"Do you trust him?" Fenn asked, his gaze piercing. "Do you trust the Chancellor with something this powerful?"

Brayden opened his mouth to respond but then closed it, his jaw tightening. He looked away, his eyes lingering on the flickering lanterns. "We don't really have a choice, do we?" he muttered.

Fenn shook his head, feeling a knot tighten in his chest. "We always have a choice, Brayden," he said softly. "We just have to be willing to make it."

Brayden didn't respond, and the silence between them grew heavy. Finally, he let out a frustrated sigh and turned towards the door. "Get some sleep, Fenn," he said over his shoulder. "You're overthinking things."

As Brayden left, Fenn turned back to the engine, his fingers tracing the lines of the containment runes. The faint red glow seemed to intensify for a moment, and Fenn felt a shiver run down his spine.

It's like it's alive, he thought, the idea both absurd and terrifying.

He moved to the back of the workbench, where an old journal lay open. It was filled with notes and sketches from previous engineers—those who had worked on the first spirit engines years ago. Fenn had been reading through it over the past few weeks, searching for anything that could explain what he was seeing now.

There, in the margins of one page, were hastily scribbled words: *Unstable containment… spirits resistant… pain triggers volatility.*

Fenn stared at the words, his mind racing. He had been trained to think of spirits as nothing more than energy—raw power to be harnessed. But what if they were more? What if the old legends were true, and the spirits were sentient in some way? What if every pulse of energy he felt in the cores wasn't just instability, but suffering?

"Why would he hide this?" Fenn murmured to himself, his fingers tightening around the edge of the journal. "Why would the Chancellor keep this from us?"

The question lingered in the air, and for the first time, Fenn felt a deep sense of dread settle over him. If the Chancellor knew about this—if he was deliberately suppressing the truth about the spirits' suffering—then what else was he hiding?

Fenn looked back at the engine, the containment runes still pulsing faintly with that ominous red glow. The light seemed almost alive now, flickering like a heartbeat—a heartbeat filled with pain.

"I have to know," Fenn whispered, his voice shaking. "I have to find out what's really going on."

He closed the journal, his heart pounding in his chest. The doubts that had been lingering at the back of his mind were now impossible to ignore. The Chancellor's assurances felt hollow, and Fenn couldn't shake the feeling that he was part of something far more dangerous than he had ever imagined.

And if he didn't act soon, it might be too late to stop it.

The air felt heavier in the heart of the forest. Lira could sense it in every breath she took, the subtle tremor beneath her feet as if the ground itself was weeping. The whispers of Elaria were no longer gentle murmurs—they had become cries of anguish, resonating through her very bones. She pressed her hand against the rough bark of a nearby tree, trying to steady herself.

"Breathe, Lira," she whispered to herself. "You have to stay strong."

But the pain in the forest was overwhelming. She could feel the pulse of the trees struggling against something dark and foreign, something unnatural that was spreading like poison. The machines of Ironhold were pushing deeper, and the spirits were growing weaker.

Lira had always felt a connection to the spirits—a bond forged through years of listening and learning. But now, that bond felt fragile, like a fraying rope on the verge of snapping. She needed help, and she knew there was only one place left to turn.

She made her way to the outer grove, where the ancient and elusive spirits dwelled—those who were older than the Fae and less inclined to intervene in the affairs of mortals. The trees grew taller and denser here, their branches intertwining to form a natural canopy that blocked out most of the sunlight. Lira felt a chill run down her spine as she stepped into the shaded grove, the air thick with an almost tangible tension.

"Elder Sylla?" Lira called softly, her voice trembling slightly.

There was no immediate response, only the rustling of leaves in the faint breeze. Lira waited, her heart pounding, until finally, the bark of one of the largest trees began to shift. A face slowly emerged from the trunk, eyes like deep pools of water, reflecting the light of centuries.

"Lira of Elaria," the spirit murmured, her voice as ancient and deep as the roots beneath them. "Why do you seek us now?"

Lira swallowed hard, taking a step closer. "Elder Sylla," she began, her voice tinged with desperation. "The forest is suffering. Ironhold's machines are advancing, and the spirits are being captured, their magic twisted into something unnatural. I—"

"We know of the pain," Sylla interrupted, her eyes narrowing slightly. "The land cries out to us, even in our silence. But what can a mortal child do against such darkness?"

"I need your help," Lira pleaded, her voice almost breaking. "The spirits are losing their strength, and my connection to them is weakening. I can't fight this alone."

Sylla's eyes darkened, her expression unreadable. "You ask much of us, mortal," she replied slowly. "The outer spirits do not easily give their trust, especially not to those who bear the blood of men."

"I know," Lira said, her voice barely a whisper. "But if we don't stand together, Elaria will fall. I can't let that happen."

Another voice emerged from the shadows—a younger spirit, her form delicate and ethereal. "Why should we help you?" she asked, her tone more curious than hostile. "You are human, and the humans of Ironhold have brought nothing but pain."

Lira turned to face the younger spirit, meeting her gaze with quiet determination. "Because I'm not like them," she said firmly. "The forest chose me as its guardian. I can feel its pain as if it were my own."

"Feeling pain does not make you one of us," Sylla murmured, her voice heavy with the weight of ages. "It is only in understanding that you may find the strength to endure it."

"Then help me understand," Lira urged, her eyes pleading. "Show me how to strengthen my bond with the forest—how to merge its magic with my own."

The spirits exchanged glances, their expressions guarded. Lira felt her heart sink. She knew she was asking for something rare and precious—something the spirits were not accustomed to sharing with mortals. But she had no other choice. She had to try.

"Please," she said softly, her voice trembling. "I'll do whatever it takes. Just… help me save Elaria."

Sylla's eyes remained fixed on Lira for a long moment, as if searching for something deep within her. Finally, she let out a sigh that seemed to reverberate through the grove. "Very well," she said quietly. "But know this, Lira of Elaria—our magic is not yours to command. If you attempt to take more than you can bear, the consequences will be dire."

"I understand," Lira replied, her voice steady despite the fear gnawing at her heart. "I'll be careful."

Sylla's branches swayed slightly, and she gestured for Lira to step closer. The younger spirit reached out, her fingers brushing against Lira's hand. Lira felt a rush of energy flow through her—a strange, otherworldly sensation that made her gasp. It was both exhilarating and terrifying, like being caught in the eye of a storm.

"Focus," Sylla instructed, her voice firm. "Feel the pulse of the forest, and let it guide you."

Lira closed her eyes, trying to steady her breathing. She could feel the spirits' magic coursing through her, intertwining with her own. But it was like trying to grasp water in her hands—it kept slipping away, leaving her grasping at nothing.

"Don't force it," the younger spirit said gently. "Listen to the whispers. Let them guide you."

Lira nodded, focusing on the faint murmur of the forest around her. She reached out with her mind, trying to merge her magic with the spirits'. For a moment, she felt a connection—a brief, fleeting spark of unity. But then, something shifted, and the magic surged uncontrollably.

"No!" Lira cried, feeling the energy slip from her grasp. The connection shattered, and she felt the backlash hit her like a physical blow. She staggered, her vision blurring as pain shot through her.

"Enough," Sylla's voice cut through the chaos, sharp and commanding. The energy dissipated, leaving Lira gasping for breath.

Lira sank to her knees, tears stinging her eyes. "I... I failed," she whispered, her voice barely audible.

Sylla watched her in silence, her expression unreadable. "You are not yet ready," she said softly. "Your heart is strong, but your spirit is still young. You seek to carry a burden that even the ancient ones struggle to bear."

"But I have to try," Lira said, her voice breaking. "I have to do something."

"Desperation can be a powerful force," Sylla replied, her tone more gentle now. "But it can also lead to ruin. You must find balance, Lira of Elaria, or you will lose yourself in the darkness."

Lira closed her eyes, feeling the crushing weight of responsibility settle over her. She had pushed herself too far, too fast, and now she was paying the price. But even in her failure, she couldn't ignore the urgency of the forest's cries.

"I'll find the balance," she whispered, more to herself than to the spirits. "I'll find a way to make this right."

The younger spirit knelt beside her, placing a hand on her shoulder. "We will be here," she said softly. "When you are ready to try again."

Lira looked up, meeting the spirit's gaze with a mixture of gratitude and determination. She wasn't alone, even if it felt that way sometimes. And she would keep trying, no matter how many times she stumbled.

"Thank you," she murmured, her voice shaky but sincere.

Sylla inclined her head, her eyes reflecting the wisdom of ages. "Go now, child of the forest," she said quietly. "And remember—strength comes not from power alone, but from understanding and patience."

Lira nodded, rising to her feet. She still had a long way to go, but at least now she had a direction. And as she left the grove, she couldn't shake the feeling that the forest was watching her, waiting to see if she could find the strength to bridge the growing chasm between hope and despair.

The borderlands between Elaria and Ironhold were a stark contrast of worlds—a place where ancient trees met newly laid roads, and where the whispers of the forest clashed with the distant rumble of machines. Fenn often came here, drawn to the edge of Ironhold's expansion where the first signs of the forest's suffering were most evident. It was here, amid the old trees and new scars, that he felt the growing weight of his doubts.

He stood silently by a twisted oak, its bark marred by deep grooves, as if it had been clawed at by unseen hands. He reached out and touched one of the scars, feeling a chill run up his arm. It was different from anything he had ever felt in the city—raw and unsettling.

"What have we done?" he muttered to himself, his voice barely audible.

"Who's there?" a voice called from further in the forest, sharp and filled with tension.

Fenn stiffened, his hand dropping to his side as he instinctively stepped back into the shadows. He peered through the dense foliage, spotting a figure kneeling on the forest floor. A girl, her shoulders hunched and her hands pressed against the ground, as if trying to draw strength from the earth itself. She looked young, her long dark hair partially hiding her face, and there was something about the way she moved—something desperate.

He took a cautious step forward, his curiosity outweighing his caution. "Are you... lost?" he called out, keeping his voice low.

The girl's head shot up, and Fenn saw her eyes—green and fierce, yet clouded with fear. She stood quickly, her posture shifting into a defensive stance.

"I'm not here to hurt you," Fenn said, raising his hands in a gesture of peace. "I just... I heard you."

"Who are you?" she demanded, her voice wavering slightly. "You're not—"

"I'm an engineer from Ironhold," Fenn replied, his words coming out almost automatically. He saw the alarm flash across her face and quickly added, "But I'm not here to report you or... or cause trouble."

The girl's expression hardened, but she didn't move. "Why should I believe you?"

Fenn hesitated, unsure of what to say. He could see that she was exhausted, her face pale and her hands trembling. He remembered the containment runes, the way they pulsed with a life of their own, and he couldn't shake the feeling that she was somehow connected to all of this.

"You're trying to help the forest, aren't you?" he asked quietly.

The girl's eyes narrowed. "Who are you?" she repeated, her voice firmer this time.

"My name is Fenn," he said, taking another cautious step forward. "I'm... I'm trying to figure out what's really going on. With Ironhold. With the spirits. I—" He paused, searching for the right words. "I don't know if I can trust what they're telling us."

The girl studied him for a moment, her eyes filled with suspicion and something else—something that looked almost like understanding. "You're doubting your own people?" she asked, her voice softer now.

Fenn let out a bitter laugh, shaking his head. "I guess I am," he admitted. "It's hard not to, after everything I've seen."

"What have you seen?" she pressed, her curiosity getting the better of her wariness.

"Things that don't make sense," Fenn replied, his voice lowering. "Spirits reacting to the machines like... like they're in pain. Runes that flare up, containment protocols that are meant to keep something suppressed. They keep telling us it's just energy, but it doesn't feel like that."

The girl's expression shifted, the suspicion in her eyes replaced by something closer to empathy. She let out a slow breath, her shoulders relaxing slightly. "My name is Lira," she said quietly. "I'm trying to stop Ironhold from destroying the forest."

"Lira," Fenn repeated, as if committing the name to memory. "You can... hear the spirits, can't you?"

She nodded, a faint sadness crossing her face. "I can. But they're getting quieter, weaker. And I can't help them—not like this."

Fenn took a step closer, his voice hesitant. "I saw you struggling just now," he said. "It looked like you were trying to... connect with them?"

"I was," Lira replied, her voice strained. "But it's not enough. My connection is too weak, and I can't do this alone. I thought if I could reach them, strengthen the bond, maybe—"

"You think the forest is alive?" Fenn interrupted, his tone more curious than dismissive.

"I know it is," Lira replied firmly, her eyes meeting his with a fierce intensity. "The spirits are a part of it, and so am I. But I'm only one person."

Fenn felt a pang of guilt at her words. He had spent years dismissing the old legends, focusing only on the machines and their schematics. But now, standing here at the edge of Ironhold's encroachment, with the weight of his doubts pressing down on him, he couldn't help but wonder if he had been blind to something important.

"What if…" Fenn began, hesitating. "What if there was a way to work together? I mean, you and… and me. I don't know if I can do much, but—"

"Why would you want to help me?" Lira asked, her voice tinged with doubt. "You're from Ironhold. You're part of the problem."

"I know," Fenn admitted, the words tasting bitter in his mouth. "But I didn't realize what we were doing. Not until recently. And now…" He looked down, feeling a strange sense of shame. "Now I can't ignore it."

Lira studied him for a long moment, her eyes searching his face for any sign of deception. Finally, she let out a sigh. "I don't know if I can trust you," she said honestly. "But I don't have many choices left."

Fenn nodded, understanding the weight of her words. "I don't know if I can trust myself," he replied, his voice barely above a whisper. "But I have to try."

They stood in silence for a moment, the forest around them eerily quiet. It was as if the entire land was holding its breath, waiting for them to decide their fates. Fenn felt the tension in his chest loosen slightly, the realization settling over him that he wasn't alone in his doubts. And maybe, just maybe, he wasn't powerless to change things.

"We're both at a crossroads," Lira said softly, her voice carrying a note of weary resignation. "If we don't act, everything will fall apart."

Fenn met her gaze, a newfound resolve hardening within him. "Then let's act," he said quietly. "Together."

Lira hesitated, but then she nodded, a faint spark of hope in her eyes. "Together," she echoed, her voice steady despite the uncertainty that lay ahead.

It wasn't a grand alliance or a perfect plan, but it was a start. And for now, that was all they could ask for.

Chapter 11
The Forest's Awakening

The air was thick with the scent of iron and the bitter tang of ozone. The distant rumble of Ironhold's machines echoed through the forest, their march a relentless drumbeat that seemed to resonate in the very roots of the trees. The forest's ancient guardians stirred uneasily, their whispers a chorus of warning and dread. At the heart of Elaria, Lira stood with her allies, her hand resting against the bark of an ancient oak, feeling the vibrations of the approaching force.

Fenn approached, his face pale and set with grim determination. "They've reached the outer groves," he reported, his voice tense. "The scouts say they're bringing more of those corrupted constructs. And… there's something else with them. A spirit bound in iron, unlike anything we've seen before."

Lira felt a chill run down her spine, her fingers tightening against the oak's bark. "A corrupted guardian?" she asked, her voice barely concealing her horror.

Fenn nodded. "It's… powerful," he admitted, his voice almost a whisper. "The scouts couldn't get close enough to see more, but they felt its presence. It's like a wound in the air."

Lira turned her gaze towards the horizon, where the distant smoke from Ironhold's march darkened the sky. She could feel the forest's pain, the twisted presence of the corrupted spirits spreading like a toxin through the land. "We need to hold them here," she said, trying to steady her voice. "If they reach the heart of Elaria, there will be nothing left to save."

Kara approached, her movements swift and graceful, the silver of her hair catching the dim light. "The Fae are ready," she said, her voice as cold and sharp as a winter wind. "But their faith in this alliance is fragile. If you falter, Guardian, the Fae will not stay."

"I won't falter," Lira replied, meeting Kara's gaze with a determination that belied her fear. "And neither will you."

Kara inclined her head, a small acknowledgment of Lira's challenge. "Let us hope your faith is not misplaced," she murmured.

Before more words could be exchanged, a low, rumbling growl echoed through the clearing. Farael materialized from the shadows, his mist-like form solidifying into that of a great wolf. His eyes, glowing faintly like distant stars, met Lira's. "The Wild Ones sense the corruption spreading," he warned, his voice a deep, resonant murmur. "They are ready to fight, but they will not be easily controlled."

"They don't need to be controlled," Lira replied, her voice firm. "They need to be guided."

Farael's ears twitched slightly, and he inclined his head. "Then guide them well, Guardian," he said. "For the storm is upon us."

Lira turned to face the gathered forces, a mix of Fae warriors, ancient spirits, and the primal, untamed Wild Ones who had answered her call. The tension in the air was palpable, every eye watching her, waiting for a sign of weakness or doubt. Lira took a deep breath, feeling the weight of their expectations press down on her shoulders.

"Ironhold is coming," she began, her voice carrying through the clearing. "They bring their machines and their corrupted spirits, driven by greed and ambition. But we are not just fighting for our survival—we are fighting for Elaria, for the balance that holds this forest together."

The murmurs of the gathered forces grew quieter, their focus sharpening on her words. Lira could see the doubt and fear in their eyes, but she could also see the spark of hope that had not yet been extinguished.

"They think they can bend this forest to their will," Lira continued, her voice gaining strength. "But we are not just trees and roots. We are spirits, we are guardians, and we are the heartbeat of this land. And today, we show Ironhold that we are not so easily broken."

A murmur of agreement rippled through the gathering, faint but growing. Lira could feel the forest's power stirring, the ancient magic awakening within the earth and the air.

Kara stepped forward, her gaze steady. "The Fae will stand with you, Guardian," she said, her voice carrying both a warning and a promise. "But remember—if you lose control, if you let the Song consume you, it will not be Ironhold that we face."

"I won't let that happen," Lira replied, though the weight of Kara's words lingered.

There was a sudden stillness in the air, a moment of quiet before the storm. Then, from the distance, the first of Ironhold's machines emerged from the treeline, their iron forms glinting in the dim light. They were grotesque, twisted things—great, lumbering constructs powered by the corrupted energy of bound spirits. The sight of them sent a shiver of rage through Lira's veins, her anger sharpening her focus.

As the machines advanced, a figure stepped forward—a hulking, corrupted spirit, its once-ethereal form now encased in iron and dark runes. It moved with a slow, deliberate grace, its presence exuding an air of menace that made the trees themselves shudder.

Lira felt her breath catch in her throat. This was not just a corrupted spirit—it was one of Elaria's ancient guardians, twisted and enslaved by Ironhold's dark magic. She could feel its pain, its anger, and its confusion, like a distant echo reverberating through the roots of the trees.

"It's time," she said softly, her voice trembling with a mix of fear and resolve.

Farael let out a low growl, his eyes narrowing. "The Wild Ones will strike when you give the signal," he said. "But know this—once the battle begins, there will be no turning back."

Lira nodded, her hand tightening around the hilt of her dagger. "I know," she replied, her voice steady. "And I'm ready."

Kara glanced at her, a faint flicker of something like respect in her eyes. "Then let the forest speak," she said quietly.

Lira raised her hand, feeling the ancient magic thrumming through her veins. The Song of the Trees was there, just beneath the surface, its melody both beautiful and terrible. She closed her eyes for a moment, focusing on the rhythm of the forest's heartbeat, and then she spoke.

"For Elaria," she whispered, her voice carrying through the clearing like a prayer.

The first battle cry rang out, and the forest erupted into motion. Spirits surged forward, their forms shimmering like moonlight on water. The Wild Ones leapt from the shadows, their eyes gleaming with primal fury. And the Fae moved with deadly grace, their weapons glinting in the dim light as they joined the fray.

Lira felt the earth tremble beneath her feet as the machines clashed with the defenders of Elaria, the sounds of metal and magic filling the air. She could feel the Song stirring within her, its power awakening with every beat of her heart. But she couldn't let it overwhelm her—not now, not when so much depended on her.

She took a deep breath, her gaze fixed on the corrupted guardian that loomed in the distance. "For Elaria," she whispered again, and then she moved, the forest's power thrumming in her veins like a storm ready to break.

The clearing had erupted into chaos. The cries of spirits clashed with the grinding roars of Ironhold's machines, their iron shells glinting in the dim light that filtered through the canopy. The air crackled with the clash of natural magic against corrupted energy, and the forest seemed to shudder with each impact. Lira darted between the twisted constructs, her senses attuned to every whisper of pain that rippled through the land.

She slashed at the legs of a smaller machine, disrupting its runes with a surge of green light. The construct faltered, its movements becoming erratic before it collapsed in a heap of smoldering metal. But there were more coming—more machines, more spirits bound in iron, their cries filling her mind with a torrent of grief and anger.

"Kara!" Lira shouted, her voice barely carrying over the cacophony of battle. "The machines—they're too many!"

Kara appeared beside her, her twin blades flashing in the dim light as she dispatched another of the corrupted constructs. Her silver eyes gleamed with fury, but there was a calculated calm in her movements. "Hold the line!" she barked, her voice sharp and commanding. "Do not let them reach the heart of the forest!"

Lira nodded, pushing down her fear as she turned to face another wave of invaders. She felt the Song of the Trees thrumming within her, its power building with each heartbeat, but it wasn't enough. Not against this. She could feel the strain in her connection to the forest, the delicate balance wavering with each spirit that was lost.

Across the battlefield, Fenn was desperately trying to disrupt the machines' runes, his face streaked with dirt and sweat. He looked up, catching Lira's eye, and for a moment, she saw the same desperation in his gaze that she felt in her heart.

"We can't hold them much longer!" Fenn called, his voice hoarse with exhaustion. "They just keep coming!"

Lira gritted her teeth, her mind racing. "We have to," she replied, forcing a conviction she didn't fully feel into her voice. "We can't let them win."

Another machine lumbered toward her, its iron limbs groaning under the strain of its corrupted power. Lira raised her hand, calling upon the magic within her, and sent a wave of green energy crashing into the machine's core. The runes flickered and sputtered, but the machine continued to advance, driven by the twisted spirit bound within.

"Lira!" Farael's voice cut through the chaos, his great form materializing beside her. "They're breaking through the eastern line! The Wild Ones can't hold them alone!"

Lira felt her heart sink. "We need to reinforce them," she said urgently. "Where's Ashen?"

"Struggling to keep the spirits from scattering," Farael replied, his voice heavy with frustration. "They're frightened, confused—torn between fighting and fleeing."

Kara appeared beside them, her expression grim. "We need to regroup," she said, her tone carrying both an order and a plea. "If the lines break, the machines will reach the heart of Elaria."

Lira glanced around, seeing the chaos and the desperation etched into every face—human, Fae, and spirit alike. She felt the weight of their lives pressing down on her, the responsibility threatening to overwhelm her. But she couldn't let that happen. Not now.

"I'll go to the eastern line," Lira said, her voice firm despite the fear gnawing at her. "Kara, keep the central line strong. Farael, rally the Wild Ones."

Kara nodded curtly, her eyes narrowing with determination. "Don't let them breach the line," she warned.

"I won't," Lira replied, though she wasn't sure she believed her own words.

As she moved towards the eastern front, the sounds of battle seemed to intensify, each clash and cry echoing in her mind like a distant storm. She could feel the spirits' fear and confusion, their pain like a knife twisting in her chest. And with each moment that passed, she felt her own magic slipping, her connection to the forest strained by the relentless assault.

When she reached the eastern line, she saw the Wild Ones fighting desperately against a new wave of machines. The great stags charged, their antlers crackling with lightning, and the mist-wolves tore at the iron constructs with fangs of spectral energy. But the machines were too many, their corrupted power overwhelming the Wild Ones' natural magic.

Lira raised her hand, calling upon the Song of the Trees, and sent a surge of green energy into the fray. The earth itself seemed to respond, roots bursting from the ground to ensnare the machines. But it wasn't enough. The constructs ripped through the roots with brutal efficiency, their iron limbs crushing everything in their path.

She felt a sharp pain in her chest as one of the stags fell, its cries of agony reverberating through the forest like a death knell. The connection between her and the forest faltered, and Lira staggered, her breath catching in her throat.

"No," she whispered, her voice breaking. "No, not again."

Fenn appeared beside her, his expression frantic. "Lira!" he shouted, grabbing her arm. "You can't keep fighting like this—it's tearing you apart!"

Lira shook her head, trying to focus. "I have to," she said, her voice shaking. "If I stop, they'll—"

"They'll break through anyway!" Fenn interrupted, his voice raw with desperation. "Your magic alone isn't enough to stop them!"

Lira felt a wave of despair wash over her, the truth of his words settling heavily in her heart. She could feel the forest crying out, its ancient magic buckling under the strain of the battle. Her power, her connection to Elaria—it wasn't enough to turn the tide.

"I don't know what else to do," she admitted, her voice barely a whisper. "I've tried everything."

Fenn's grip on her arm tightened, and she could see the determination in his eyes, a fierce resolve that mirrored her own. "You're not alone in this," he said quietly. "We're all fighting with you."

Lira met his gaze, seeing the fear and the hope mingling in his eyes. She felt a spark of something stir within her—a reminder that this wasn't just her battle. It was their battle, their fight for the future of Elaria.

"We need a new plan," Fenn continued, his voice steady. "We can't keep throwing everything at them and hoping it's enough. We need to be smarter than that."

Lira nodded slowly, a sense of clarity cutting through the haze of her fear and exhaustion. "We need to disrupt their power source," she said, her voice gaining strength. "If we can cut off the corrupted energy driving the machines, we might have a chance."

Fenn's eyes widened slightly, and he nodded, his expression filled with renewed purpose. "Then let's find a way to do that," he said firmly. "Together."

As they turned to face the battle once more, Lira felt a flicker of hope amidst the chaos. The odds were overwhelming, and the cost of failure was unthinkable. But for the first time, she felt a glimmer of possibility—a chance to turn the tide.

And she knew that as long as they fought together, they had a chance.

The forest was a battlefield, and every heartbeat felt like a countdown. Lira's breaths were shallow and quick as she crouched behind a massive root, its surface rough and ancient beneath her fingers. The chaos of battle raged around her—echoes of cries, the clash of metal and magic, and the relentless rumble of Ironhold's corrupted machines. She could feel the land's pain, its desperation radiating from the trees and roots.

Beside her, Fenn was catching his breath, dirt and sweat streaking his face. He looked up, his eyes scanning the horizon with a frantic intensity. "It's near," he muttered, half to himself. "If I'm right… it has to be close."

"Fenn," Lira said, her voice steady despite the storm inside her, "we need to move. Where's the final obelisk?"

He took a deep breath and turned to her, his eyes sharp with purpose. "It's beyond the old clearing," he said. "Just west of here. It was buried centuries ago, hidden beneath the roots of an ancient oak. The obelisk's power could be the key to stopping the flow of corrupted energy, but—"

"But getting there won't be easy," Lira finished, her voice tight with resolve. She glanced out at the battlefield, her gaze lingering on the towering machines cutting a swath through their forces. The corrupted constructs loomed like monstrous shadows, their movements precise and methodical, as if guided by an unseen hand.

Kara emerged from the shadows, her face etched with exhaustion but her eyes bright with defiance. "You have a plan?" she asked, her voice terse.

Lira nodded, her expression grim. "The final Lost Obelisk is just beyond the old clearing. If we can reach it, we can disrupt Ironhold's power source."

Kara's eyes narrowed. "And you're sure about this?" she pressed, her tone skeptical but hopeful.

"Not entirely," Lira admitted. "But if there's a chance it could work, we have to take it."

Kara studied her for a moment, then nodded curtly. "The Fae will cover your advance," she said, her voice firm. "But once we break through, you're on your own."

"Thank you, Kara," Lira said, sincerity lacing her words.

"Don't thank me yet," Kara replied, her voice carrying both warning and resolve. "Just don't get yourself killed."

Lira met her gaze, a silent understanding passing between them. Then she turned back to Fenn, her mind racing. "How far is it?" she asked.

"Not far," Fenn replied, glancing over his shoulder as if expecting the machines to catch up to them at any moment. "But we'll have to cross the main battlefield to get there."

Lira's jaw tightened. The battlefield was swarming with enemies—corrupted constructs, soldiers loyal to Ironhold, and twisted spirits bound in iron. The path to the obelisk was fraught with danger, but she couldn't let that stop her. Not now.

Farael materialized beside them, his mist-like form shifting with the breeze. His eyes gleamed with a quiet intensity, his voice a low murmur. "The Wild Ones sense your resolve," he said. "They will clear a path, but only for a short time. You must move quickly."

"We will," Lira promised. She took a deep breath, feeling the ancient power of the forest thrumming beneath her fingertips. She turned to Fenn, meeting his gaze. "Stay close," she instructed. "We move as one."

Fenn nodded, his expression resolute. "I'm with you," he said, his voice steady despite the fear in his eyes.

Lira raised her hand, signaling the others. Kara's warriors moved into position, their blades and magic gleaming in the half-light. The spirits whispered in the trees, their voices a chorus of ancient warnings and hopes. Lira took one last breath, steeling herself for what was to come.

"For Elaria," she whispered, her voice barely a breath.

Kara glanced at her, a faint smirk tugging at the corners of her lips. "For Elaria," she echoed, her tone carrying a hint of challenge.

Lira surged forward, and the world exploded into motion around her. The Wild Ones roared as they charged into the fray, their spectral forms cutting through the ranks of Ironhold's forces. The ground seemed to tremble beneath their fury, and for a brief moment, it felt as if the forest itself was fighting alongside them.

Lira and Fenn moved through the chaos, their path illuminated by the flashes of magic and the glint of steel. Lira's heart pounded in her chest, every step a race against time. She could feel the weight of the forest's fate pressing down on her, every breath a reminder of what was at stake.

"There!" Fenn shouted, pointing towards a distant clearing where the old oak loomed, its roots twisting and ancient. "That's it!"

Lira's eyes locked onto their destination, a surge of determination flooding her veins. "We're almost there," she urged, her voice carrying a desperate edge.

But the way was not clear. A massive construct, its iron limbs etched with dark runes, moved to block their path. The corrupted spirit within it let out a guttural roar, its eyes burning with a twisted hatred. Lira felt the creature's pain and anger radiating through the air, and for a moment, it almost overwhelmed her.

"Keep moving!" Fenn yelled, his voice cutting through the fog of dread that threatened to consume her.

Lira gritted her teeth and pushed forward, calling upon the Song of the Trees. The earth responded, roots bursting from the ground to entangle the construct's limbs. The creature struggled against its bonds, its iron frame groaning under the strain. Lira could feel the strain in her connection to the forest, the Song's power both beautiful and terrible.

"We don't have much time!" Fenn urged, his eyes wide with urgency.

"I know!" Lira replied, her voice strained with the effort of maintaining the magic.

The construct tore free from the roots, its rage palpable. But before it could strike, Kara's voice rang out like a blade cutting through the darkness. "Now!" she commanded, and her warriors unleashed a barrage of magic and arrows, driving the construct back just enough for Lira and Fenn to slip past.

They reached the clearing, the ancient oak towering above them like a silent sentinel. The final Lost Obelisk lay hidden beneath its roots, its power humming faintly in the air.

Fenn knelt beside the massive roots, his hands trembling as he began to uncover the ancient stone. "This is it," he murmured, his voice filled with awe and urgency. "If we can activate the obelisk, we can disrupt the flow of corrupted energy."

Lira placed her hand against the obelisk's surface, feeling the ancient power stirring within it. The fate of the forest rested in their hands, and she knew that there was no turning back.

"Do it," she said quietly, her voice filled with resolve. "We're out of time."

Chapter 12
Limits and Choices

Lira approached Elder Ashen's grove with quick, purposeful strides, her frustration burning hotter with each step. The grove seemed darker than usual, the towering trees casting long shadows that twisted and intertwined across the ground. The familiar whispers of the forest were muted, replaced by an uneasy silence that set Lira's nerves on edge.

She found Elder Ashen standing at the center of the grove, his ancient branches outstretched as if cradling the twilight sky. His bark was worn and rough, the deep lines etched into his form like scars. Lira had always felt a sense of awe in his presence, but today, all she felt was anger.

"Elder Ashen," Lira called, trying to keep her voice steady. "I need to speak with you."

The great oak remained still for a moment before his branches swayed slightly, a sigh of wood groaning under unseen weight. "Lira," he greeted, his voice deep and weary. "What troubles you, child?"

Lira clenched her fists, trying to hold back the wave of frustration that threatened to spill over. "Why won't you act?" she demanded, her voice sharper than she intended. "The forest is suffering, the spirits are fading, and Ironhold keeps pushing further into Elaria. I'm doing everything I can, but it's not enough. I need your help!"

Elder Ashen's branches creaked, his leaves rustling softly. "Patience, child," he replied, his voice a deep, resonant murmur. "There is a time for all things."

"Patience?" Lira repeated, her anger rising. "How can you ask for patience when Ironhold is destroying everything? You keep telling me to wait, to listen, but the forest doesn't have time to wait!"

Elder Ashen's silence in response was almost deafening. Lira could feel her frustration boiling over, and she took a step closer, her fists trembling.

"You have the power to stop this," she insisted, her voice shaking with urgency. "But all you do is stand here, watching while everything falls apart. Why?"

Elder Ashen's leaves rustled again, more like a weary sigh this time. His voice was heavy with an unspoken burden when he finally replied. "There are... things you do not yet understand, Lira."

"Then explain them to me!" Lira nearly shouted, her voice breaking. "If there's something holding you back, something I don't know, then tell me. I deserve to know why I'm fighting this battle alone!"

For a long moment, Elder Ashen said nothing. Lira felt her anger start to shift into desperation, the weight of her struggle pressing down on her like a physical force. When he finally spoke, his voice was quiet—almost mournful.

"There is an ancient vow that binds me," Elder Ashen confessed, his words slow and deliberate. "A promise made in the aftermath of the Sacred Pact."

Lira frowned, her frustration momentarily giving way to confusion. "The Sacred Pact?" she echoed, her voice barely above a whisper. "What do you mean?"

"The Pact was made long ago, in a time when humans and spirits walked together," Elder Ashen explained, his branches swaying gently as he spoke. "But that trust was shattered by betrayal, and the balance between our realms was broken. To preserve what remained, a vow was made—one that prevents the ancient spirits from intervening directly in the affairs of humans."

Lira felt a chill run down her spine. "A vow?" she repeated, her voice trembling slightly. "But… why? Why would you make such a promise?"

"To protect what little harmony was left," Elder Ashen replied softly. "The Sacred Pact was meant to ensure that neither side would dominate the other—that humans and spirits would coexist in balance. But when that balance was broken, the spirits withdrew, and those of us who remained took an oath to never again interfere in mortal affairs."

Lira took a step back, the weight of his words sinking in. "And if you break that vow?" she asked, her voice barely a whisper.

Elder Ashen's branches trembled slightly, the creaking of wood echoing through the grove. "To break the vow would be to invite chaos upon both our realms," he said quietly. "The consequences would be dire, not only for me but for all of Elaria. The Breath of Elaria would be disrupted beyond repair, and the ancient forces that keep the balance would turn against us."

Lira felt her throat tighten, her mind racing. "So you're saying… you can't help me?" she asked, her voice strained with desperation.

"I cannot intervene directly," Elder Ashen replied, his voice filled with regret. "My power is bound by the vow, and even if I wished to act, the Breath of Elaria is weakening. My strength fades with it."

Lira shook her head, her frustration giving way to a sense of helplessness. "But there has to be something you can do," she pleaded. "Something you haven't told me."

"There is only one path left to you, child," Elder Ashen said softly. "You must find a way to strengthen your bond with the forest, to draw upon the spirits and unite them. Only then will you have the power to resist Ironhold's influence."

"But I've tried," Lira whispered, her voice breaking. "I've tried, and I've failed."

"Failure is not the end, Lira," Elder Ashen replied, his tone gentle despite the gravity of his words. "It is only a step on the path. You have the heart of a guardian, and the forest chose you for a reason. But you must find the balance within yourself before you can find it in the world."

Lira looked down, her eyes stinging with unshed tears. "How am I supposed to do that?" she asked quietly, feeling the crushing weight of responsibility pressing down on her.

"Listen to the whispers, and trust in yourself," Elder Ashen said, his voice like a soft breeze. "The path is not always clear, but you are not alone. The forest is with you, even in its silence."

Lira closed her eyes, taking a slow, shaky breath. She wanted to argue, to demand more answers, but she knew that Elder Ashen had told her everything he could. His hands were tied by ancient promises, and his power was fading along with the Breath of Elaria.

"I'll keep trying," Lira whispered, her voice barely audible. "But… if I can't find the strength, then—"

"You will," Elder Ashen interrupted gently. "You are stronger than you know, child. Do not lose hope."

Lira nodded slowly, feeling the weight of his words settle over her. She didn't have all the answers, but at least now she understood why Elder Ashen couldn't help her. And as frustrating as it was, she knew she couldn't blame him for honoring a vow that had been made long before her time.

"Thank you, Elder," she said quietly, her voice steady despite the lingering uncertainty in her heart.

"Go now, Lira," Elder Ashen replied, his voice filled with a deep, ancient sadness. "And remember—you are not alone in this fight. The forest watches over you, even when the way forward seems unclear."

Lira turned to leave, her steps slow and heavy. She still felt the crushing weight of her responsibilities, but at least now she understood why Elder Ashen had held back. It wasn't out of indifference or reluctance—it was because he was bound by forces older than either of them.

As she walked away from the grove, the whispers of the forest began to stir once more, a faint murmur of hope amid the growing darkness.

The Ironhold factory buzzed with relentless activity, the air thick with the scent of oil and the rhythmic pounding of machinery. Engineers and workers moved about, focused and efficient, their faces set in expressions of purpose. But for Fenn, the familiar sounds felt distorted, as if he were hearing them from a great distance. The deeper he ventured into the heart of the factory, the more he felt the weight of the spirits' suffering pressing down on him.

"Fenn!" Brayden's voice cut through the din, pulling him back to the present. Brayden was waving him over, standing next to one of the newest engines. "There you are. I've been looking for you everywhere."

"What's going on?" Fenn asked, forcing himself to keep his voice steady.

"The Chancellor wants to see how these new models are performing," Brayden replied, gesturing to the gleaming metal of the engine beside him. "Apparently, there's been a breakthrough with the containment runes. They're supposed to be more stable, more efficient at extracting energy from the spirits."

"More stable?" Fenn echoed, the words tasting bitter on his tongue. He turned to the engine, his eyes tracing the lines of runes that spiraled around its core. They glowed faintly, a cold, unnatural light that made his skin crawl.

"That's what they say," Brayden confirmed, giving Fenn a nudge with his elbow. "Come on, don't look so grim. This is what we've been working towards, right?"

Fenn didn't respond. He felt a knot tightening in his chest, and the distant, almost imperceptible cries of the spirits seemed to grow louder in his mind. He turned to the engineer overseeing the demonstration, a man named Rylis, who was adjusting the controls with an air of confidence.

"Rylis," Fenn called, his voice strained. "What's different about these new models?"

Rylis looked up, flashing Fenn a smile that didn't reach his eyes. "We've made some modifications to the containment matrix," he explained. "The new runes are designed to prevent any… volatility from the spirits. Keeps them in line and extracts their energy more efficiently."

"Keeps them in line?" Fenn repeated, the knot in his chest tightening further. "What does that mean, exactly?"

"It means no more outbursts, no more interference," Rylis said casually, as if discussing a minor mechanical adjustment. "The spirits don't like being contained, and sometimes their resistance disrupts the energy flow. The new runes suppress that resistance."

"Suppress?" Fenn's voice came out sharper than he intended. "You mean… you're suppressing their pain?"

Rylis shrugged, not noticing the strain in Fenn's voice. "Call it what you like," he replied. "All I care about is that the output is stable."

"Stable?" Fenn took a step closer to the engine, his eyes narrowing. "How do you know it's stable?"

Rylis chuckled, clearly amused by Fenn's concern. "Why don't you see for yourself?" he said, his fingers dancing over the controls. "We're about to power it up."

Fenn felt a cold sweat break out on the back of his neck. He opened his mouth to protest, to demand more information, but the words caught in his throat. He watched helplessly as Rylis activated the engine, the runes flaring brighter.

A low hum filled the room, vibrating through the metal floor. The engine's core began to glow, and Fenn could almost feel the energy being siphoned from the captured spirit within. He clenched his fists, trying to block out the sensation, but the cries were getting louder, sharper, like nails being driven into his skull.

"There we go," Rylis said, nodding approvingly at the readout. "See? Perfectly stable."

But all Fenn could see was the pulsing light in the runes, the way it seemed to shudder with each beat, as if the engine itself were alive. He pressed a hand to his temple, trying to clear his head, but the cries only grew more insistent.

"Do you hear that?" Fenn asked, his voice barely more than a whisper.

"Hear what?" Brayden replied, looking at him with mild confusion.

"That sound," Fenn insisted, his voice rising slightly. "The… the spirit. It's… it's crying."

Brayden and Rylis exchanged a glance, and then Rylis laughed, shaking his head. "You've been working too hard, Fenn," he said dismissively. "It's just the hum of the engine."

"It's not just the engine!" Fenn snapped, his frustration boiling over. "Can't you feel it? The spirit—it's in pain!"

"Pain?" Brayden repeated, looking genuinely baffled. "Fenn, these are just… resources. You can't think of them as—"

"They're not just resources!" Fenn shouted, his voice echoing through the room. "They're alive! And we're… we're torturing them!"

The room fell silent, the other engineers turning to stare at him. Rylis raised an eyebrow, his expression shifting from amusement to something colder. "Careful, Fenn," he warned. "You're starting to sound like one of those spirit sympathizers."

"I…" Fenn felt his throat tighten, his chest heaving with the weight of his words. He looked at Brayden, searching for some sign of understanding, but all he saw was confusion and concern.

"Fenn, what's going on with you?" Brayden asked quietly. "You're not making any sense."

"I'm…" Fenn struggled to find the right words, but the cries were drowning out his thoughts. "I can't… I can't be a part of this."

Rylis sighed, shaking his head. "If you're having second thoughts, Fenn, maybe you should take some time off," he suggested, his tone edged with thinly veiled irritation. "Get your head straight."

"Time off?" Fenn echoed, feeling a hollow laugh bubble up inside him. "Is that your solution? Just… walk away and pretend this isn't happening?"

Rylis's eyes narrowed. "You need to get a grip, Fenn," he said coldly. "The Chancellor expects results, and if you're not on board—"

"I don't care about the Chancellor!" Fenn shouted, the words escaping before he could stop them. "I care about what we're doing—what we're... what we're destroying!"

There was a stunned silence, and Fenn felt the weight of his outburst settle over him like a lead blanket. He could see the shock in Brayden's eyes, the anger in Rylis's face, and he knew he had crossed a line.

"I..." Fenn took a step back, his hands trembling. "I need to get out of here."

Without waiting for a response, he turned and stumbled out of the room, his heart pounding in his chest. He could still hear the cries in his mind, echoing like a relentless drumbeat. The sound followed him as he left the factory, his thoughts racing and his doubts solidifying into something he couldn't ignore.

As Fenn stepped outside into the cold night air, he took a deep, shuddering breath. He knew he couldn't keep doing this—couldn't keep pretending that everything was fine. He was at a crossroads, and the path he chose next would change everything.

For the first time, he wasn't sure if he had the courage to keep following the road that Ironhold had laid out for him.

Lira was kneeling at the edge of the Outer Grove, her fingers pressed into the damp earth, trying desperately to reconnect with the Breath of Elaria. The ground felt colder than usual, the soil resisting her attempts to draw on its strength. The once vibrant whispers of the forest were barely a murmur now, thin and scattered like echoes lost in the wind.

She closed her eyes, focusing all her energy on reaching out to the spirits. But instead of the warm, familiar presence she had come to rely on, she felt only emptiness—a cold void that left her heart pounding with dread.

"No, no, no…" she whispered, shaking her head as if that would dispel the growing sense of doom. "Elaria, please… I'm still here. I need you."

Suddenly, a sharp pain lanced through her chest, knocking the breath from her lungs. Lira gasped, clutching at her heart, feeling the once steady pulse of the forest falter violently. It was as if something was ripping the connection from her, pulling it away piece by piece.

"Lira," a voice echoed faintly in her mind—Elder Ashen's voice, strained and distant. "You must—"

But the connection shattered, and Lira cried out as a wave of energy crashed through her. She felt the world tilt, her vision blurring as she struggled to keep her grip on the earth beneath her. She could hear the distant hum of the engines, their relentless thrum resonating like a drumbeat in her head.

"Elder Ashen!" she called, her voice breaking. "Please, I—"

But there was no response. She couldn't feel him anymore—couldn't feel the ancient tree spirit's presence guiding her, grounding her. It was as if he had been snuffed out like a dying flame.

"No," Lira choked, her nails digging into the soil. "This can't be happening…"

A voice interrupted her thoughts—sharp and cold. "You feel it too, don't you?"

Lira looked up, her vision still swimming. A figure was standing at the edge of the grove, half-shrouded in shadows. Fenn stepped forward, his face pale and his eyes dark with unease. He was holding something in his hands—a small, glowing device that emitted a faint, pulsing light.

"You…" Lira breathed, her voice filled with a mixture of recognition and confusion. "Fenn?"

"Lira," Fenn said softly, as if saying her name would somehow soften the weight of what was happening. "I didn't realize… until now…"

"What's happening?" Lira demanded, trying to steady herself. "What are you doing?"

Fenn shook his head, his voice thick with regret. "It's not me," he said quietly. "It's the engines. They're—"

"They're ripping the Breath of Elaria apart," Lira finished, her voice barely more than a whisper. "I can feel it."

Fenn took another step closer, his hands tightening around the device. "The containment runes are supposed to stabilize the energy," he explained, his tone laced with uncertainty. "But instead, they're... amplifying it. The spirits' pain is... it's feeding back into the engines, creating a—"

"A backlash," Lira finished, realization dawning on her. "That's why I can't... why I can't reach them."

"Yes," Fenn admitted, his voice breaking slightly. "I think... I think the engines are disrupting the entire balance of the forest. And if they keep going—"

"It'll be irreversible," Lira whispered, her heart sinking. "Not just to the spirits, but to me too."

Fenn looked at her, his eyes filled with a desperation that mirrored her own. "Lira," he said, his voice barely more than a whisper, "I didn't want this. I swear, I—"

"I know," Lira replied, cutting him off. "But wanting to stop it isn't enough, Fenn. We have to *do* something."

Fenn nodded, swallowing hard. "I... I need your help," he admitted, his voice trembling. "I can't fix this alone."

Lira felt the weight of his words settle over her like a lead blanket. She had spent so long fighting Ironhold, seeing them as the enemy, but now here was someone from within their ranks, standing in front of her and asking for help. It was almost too much to process.

"What can we do?" she asked, forcing herself to keep her voice steady. "How do we stop this?"

Fenn glanced down at the device in his hands, his fingers trembling slightly. "The engines are linked through these," he explained. "They're... like conduits, amplifying the energy flow. If we can disrupt them—turn them off, or overload them—it might be enough to break the feedback loop."

"Overload them?" Lira repeated, her eyes narrowing. "Won't that be dangerous?"

"Yes," Fenn admitted, his voice heavy with guilt. "But right now, the engines are tearing the spirits apart. We don't have a choice."

Lira closed her eyes, taking a deep breath. She could still feel the echoes of the forest's pain reverberating through her, each beat like a hammer striking her heart. The thought of causing more damage made her feel sick, but doing nothing was no longer an option.

"Okay," she said finally, her voice firm. "What do we need to do?"

Fenn looked at her, his expression a mixture of relief and fear. "We need to get inside Ironhold," he explained. "The main control hub is heavily guarded, but if we can find a way past the defenses—"

"We'll figure it out," Lira interrupted, determination hardening in her voice. "We don't have time to be cautious."

Fenn hesitated for a moment, and then he nodded, his eyes filled with a grim resolve. "I'll help you," he said quietly. "But if this doesn't work…"

"It will work," Lira replied, her voice unwavering. "It has to."

For a moment, they stood in silence, the weight of their decision settling over them. The wind whispered through the grove, carrying with it the faintest echo of the spirits' cries—desperate and pleading.

Lira took a deep breath, steeling herself for what was to come. She knew that the path ahead was dangerous, and the consequences of failure were unthinkable. But she also knew that if they didn't act now, the damage would become irreversible—not just to the spirits, but to everything she held dear.

"We're running out of time," Lira said softly, turning to face Fenn. "Are you ready?"

Fenn nodded, his jaw set with determination. "Let's go," he replied, his voice steady despite the fear lurking beneath it.

Together, they turned towards the edge of the grove, the weight of their choices pressing down on them like a heavy storm cloud. They were at the brink of something terrible, and the only way forward was through the heart of the storm.

Chapter 13
Lines in the Sand

The Alchemical Nexus loomed above Lira, its iron walls pulsating with a faint, dark energy that seemed to resonate with the corrupted earth beneath her feet. The weight of centuries pressed down on her shoulders, a heavy, suffocating presence that seemed to whisper of failures past. But beneath that darkness, Lira could feel another rhythm—something deeper, older, and stronger. The Song of the Trees thrummed just beneath the surface, waiting to be called forth.

Lira took a deep breath, feeling the cool air fill her lungs. She closed her eyes, trying to shut out the distant cries of battle and the relentless hum of Ironhold's machines. Instead, she focused on the whispers of the spirits, the ancient melodies that had been carried by the trees for generations. The ground beneath her seemed to pulse in time with her heartbeat, a silent promise of what was to come.

"This is madness," Fenn's voice broke through the heavy silence, his tone filled with a mixture of fear and desperation. He was standing a few feet away, his eyes wide with uncertainty. "Lira, if you invoke the Song without control—"

"I know the risks," Lira interrupted, her voice barely above a whisper. She didn't open her eyes, didn't let her focus waver. She couldn't afford to. "But this is the only way."

Fenn took a step closer, his voice trembling. "There has to be another way. We can still—"

"There isn't," Lira replied, her voice firm despite the storm raging inside her. She turned to face him, her eyes meeting his. "If we don't stop the Chancellor here, it's over. For the forest, for the spirits—for all of us."

Fenn's expression tightened, his hands clenching into fists at his sides. He wanted to argue, to fight against the inevitability of what was coming, but he couldn't find the words. Instead, he took a deep breath and nodded, his voice barely more than a whisper. "Then I'll stand with you," he said quietly. "No matter what happens."

Lira felt a surge of gratitude, and she gave him a brief, tight smile. "Thank you, Fenn," she said softly.

But before she could say more, another voice cut through the silence, cold and mocking. "You really think this will work, don't you?" The Chancellor's voice rang out from the shadows, his tone filled with cruel amusement. He stepped forward, his dark robes rustling as he moved, his presence like a shadow spreading across the chamber.

"You think you can save them?" he continued, his voice dripping with disdain. "With your ancient spells and your childish hope?"

Lira felt a flicker of anger, but she forced it down, focusing instead on the power thrumming beneath her feet. "This isn't about hope," she said quietly. "It's about balance. Something you've forgotten."

The Chancellor's smile widened, his eyes gleaming with something dark and twisted. "Balance?" he repeated, his voice almost mocking. "Balance is an illusion—a lie told by those too weak to seize the power that is rightfully theirs."

"You're wrong," Lira replied, her voice steady despite the fear gnawing at her. "Power isn't something you take—it's something you protect."

The Chancellor let out a low, mirthless laugh. "Protect?" he sneered. "You talk about protection as if you have the power to save anything. You're nothing but a relic, a fading echo of a world that no longer exists."

Lira took a deep breath, feeling the Song of the Trees stirring within her. It was a quiet hum, a distant melody that seemed to resonate with the very roots of the earth. She knew that invoking the Song meant risking everything—her life, her soul, and the fragile connection she held with the spirits. But there was no turning back now.

"This world doesn't belong to you," she said firmly, her voice carrying an edge of defiance. "It never did."

The Chancellor's expression darkened, his eyes narrowing. "You're a fool," he hissed, his voice laced with contempt. "And you will die like one."

Lira felt the ground beneath her shift, the vibrations intensifying as the Song's melody grew stronger. She could feel the ancient power flowing through her veins, a force that was both beautiful and terrible. It was like trying to hold back a storm, the energy swirling within her threatening to break free at any moment.

"Maybe I am a fool," she admitted, her voice barely more than a whisper. "But I'd rather be a fool fighting for something real than a coward hiding behind lies."

The Chancellor's eyes flashed with anger, and he raised his hand, dark energy crackling at his fingertips. "Enough of this," he snarled. "If you will not yield, then I will end this farce myself."

Lira closed her eyes, shutting out the Chancellor's voice and the fear that threatened to overwhelm her. She focused on the Song, letting its melody guide her, feeling the ancient magic weaving through her thoughts. The trees seemed to whisper in the back of her mind, their voices urging her to trust in the power she had been given.

She took a deep breath and began to sing.

The words were not her own, but they came to her as if she had known them all her life. They were the words of the forest, the memories of the ancient trees that had stood for centuries, watching over the land. The melody was soft at first, barely more than a whisper, but it grew stronger with each breath, resonating with the very roots of the earth.

The air around her seemed to vibrate with the power of the Song, the melody echoing through the chamber like a distant, mournful prayer. Lira could feel the spirits stirring in response, their presence like a quiet breath against her skin. The ancient power flowed through her veins, a connection that transcended time and space.

The Chancellor's expression shifted from anger to something closer to fear, his eyes widening as he felt the power of the Song. "What are you doing?" he demanded, his voice laced with desperation. "Stop this!"

But Lira didn't stop. She let the Song carry her, her voice rising and falling in time with the ancient melody. She could feel the roots of the trees beneath her, their presence like a steady heartbeat, and she knew that she was not alone. The spirits were with her, the forest was with her, and together, they were stronger than the darkness that threatened to consume them.

As the final notes of the Song echoed through the chamber, Lira felt the ground beneath her tremble, the air vibrating with the power of the ancient melody. She opened her eyes, meeting the Chancellor's gaze with unwavering resolve.

"This ends now," she said, her voice carrying the weight of her resolve.

The Chancellor's face twisted with fury, and he raised his hand, dark energy surging towards her. But the Song's power was stronger, a force that flowed through Lira like a river, washing away the darkness that sought to drown her.

And as the world seemed to hold its breath, Lira felt a quiet certainty settle over her—a resolve that was stronger than her fear, stronger than her anger. She had invoked the Song of the Trees, and she knew that there was no turning back now.

For the forest, for the spirits, and for the future of Elaria.

The melody of the Song filled the air, its ancient notes resonating with the walls of the Nexus and the very roots of the city beneath it. Lira felt the power vibrating through her bones, the connection between herself and the spirits growing stronger with every passing moment. Her voice carried the Song, her words woven into the very fabric of the forest's memory, and she could feel the spirits stirring in response.

As the last haunting note of the Song echoed through the chamber, Lira opened her eyes. She watched as tendrils of green energy spiraled outward from her, weaving through the machinery, the iron walls, and the heavy chains that bound the spirits. She could feel the Song's power thrumming through her veins, a wild and unpredictable force that was no longer entirely under her control.

The air around her seemed to shimmer, the energy gathering like a storm waiting to break. She saw the first chain dissolve into mist, and then another. The spirits, trapped within Ironhold's machines, shuddered as the invisible bonds that held them began to weaken.

The Chancellor's face twisted with fury and fear. "No!" he shouted, his voice laced with panic. He raised his hand, dark energy crackling around him. "You think this changes anything? I will not let you destroy what I've built!"

"It's not about destroying," Lira replied, her voice steady despite the chaos around her. "It's about setting things right."

The Chancellor hurled a bolt of dark energy towards her, but the Song's magic enveloped Lira like a protective shield, absorbing the attack and dissipating it into the air. She didn't flinch, her focus unbroken as she continued to channel the Song. She felt the ancient melody resonate with the spirits, their cries of anguish turning into a harmony of hope.

All around her, the machines began to stutter and groan as their power sources—corrupted spirits—were freed from their enslavement. The runes carved into the iron shells flickered and dimmed, their dark glow fading as the spirits pulled away, their bonds dissolving into ethereal mist.

One by one, the machines collapsed, their iron shells crumbling to the ground as the spirits escaped. The air was thick with mist, shimmering with the essence of ancient souls finally released from their torment. Lira felt their gratitude and their pain mingling with the magic of the Song, a bittersweet harmony that made her heart ache.

"You... you can't do this!" The Chancellor's voice was shaking now, his composure slipping as he watched his empire unravel before his eyes. He turned to Fenn, his voice desperate. "You! Stop her! You're one of us!"

Fenn's expression was one of grim determination. He shook his head, his voice steady. "Not anymore," he said. "This isn't the future I want to build."

The Chancellor's face contorted with rage, and he raised his hand to strike at Fenn. But before he could, a spectral form materialized between them—one of the spirits, its eyes glowing with a fierce light. It let out a keening wail, and the Chancellor stumbled back, his attack faltering.

"This isn't over!" he snarled, his voice filled with venom. "You don't understand what you're doing—what you're risking!"

Lira felt the Song's power reach its crescendo, the ancient melody weaving through the Nexus and the city beyond. The walls began to tremble, cracks spidering across the iron and stone as the magic destabilized the foundations of the city. The Alchemical Nexus, once a monument to Ironhold's power, was now crumbling under the weight of its own corruption.

"The spirits are free," Lira said, her voice soft but resolute. "And your control over them is broken."

The Chancellor's eyes widened, and for a moment, there was a flicker of something like fear in his gaze. "You don't know what you've unleashed," he hissed. "This power—it's beyond your control!"

Lira took a deep breath, feeling the weight of the Song's power within her. "It's not about control," she said quietly. "It's about trust."

As she spoke, the spirits continued to break free, their chains dissolving into mist and their forms becoming more solid, more real. The room was filled with their ethereal presence, their once-silenced voices now a chorus of freedom and hope. Lira could feel their gratitude washing over her, a wave of warmth that made her eyes sting with unshed tears.

The ground beneath them began to quake, the vibrations growing stronger as the Nexus destabilized. Fenn took a step towards Lira, his expression one of concern. "Lira, the city—"

"I know," Lira replied, her voice heavy with the weight of what was happening. "We have to leave—now."

The Chancellor's voice cut through the growing chaos, his tone desperate and filled with a dark resolve. "If I fall, I'll take you all with me!" he shouted, his hands raised as dark energy crackled around him. He began to chant, his voice laced with a twisted incantation.

But before he could complete the spell, one of the spirits surged forward, its form shimmering with a brilliant light. It let out a cry, and the dark energy around the Chancellor dissipated, the spell broken. He staggered, his eyes wide with disbelief and fury.

"No!" he screamed, his voice breaking. "I am Ironhold! I—"

The spirit's light enveloped him, and the Chancellor's scream was cut off, his form dissolving into the mist. The light faded, and the spirit turned to Lira, its eyes filled with a quiet sadness.

"Thank you," it whispered, its voice barely more than a breath. And then it, too, dissolved into the air, leaving the room eerily silent.

Lira took a shaky breath, her legs feeling weak beneath her. The Song's magic was beginning to fade, the ancient melody settling into a quiet hum in the back of her mind. She could feel the exhaustion creeping in, the strain of what she had done weighing heavily on her.

Fenn placed a hand on her shoulder, his voice filled with quiet urgency. "We have to go," he said. "The city—"

Lira nodded, her voice barely audible. "Let's go."

As they turned to leave, the ground beneath them trembled once more, the walls of the Nexus cracking and crumbling. Lira glanced back one last time, seeing the mist-filled chamber and the shattered remnants of Ironhold's power. It was a sight both tragic and beautiful, a reminder of what had been lost and what had been saved.

And as the city began to collapse around them, Lira felt a quiet resolve settle over her—a promise to the spirits and to herself that she would honor their sacrifice, and protect the fragile balance they had fought so hard to restore.

The remnants of the Song lingered in the air, a soft, fading melody that resonated through the crumbling walls of the Nexus. Lira stood at its center, the ancient magic still thrumming through her veins, but it no longer felt like a comforting presence. Instead, it was a storm inside her, a force that pulled at her with every breath she took.

She could feel her connection to the forest weakening, the roots of Elaria slipping from her grasp like sand through her fingers. Every heartbeat felt more distant, every whisper from the spirits more faint. The Song was calling her, pulling her further away from the world she had known and the people she had sworn to protect.

Fenn was at her side, his face etched with concern. "Lira," he said, his voice trembling. "What's happening? You're—"

"I can't hold it," she whispered, her voice barely more than a breath. "The Song… it's taking me with it."

Fenn's eyes widened in alarm. He reached for her hand, gripping it tightly, as if his touch could keep her anchored to reality. "Then stop," he urged, his voice laced with desperation. "You have to stop, Lira!"

"I can't," Lira replied, her voice filled with quiet resignation. She could feel the ancient magic swirling within her, its melody echoing through her thoughts, drowning out everything else. "If I stop now, the corruption will return. Everything we've fought for—everything the spirits sacrificed—it'll all be in vain."

"There has to be another way," Fenn insisted, his voice breaking with emotion. "We'll find it together—just hold on."

Lira shook her head, a sad smile tugging at the corners of her lips. She could see the fear in Fenn's eyes, the same fear that gripped her heart, but she knew what needed to be done. The

Song was not just a melody—it was a choice, a final act of defiance against the darkness that had consumed Ironhold.

"There isn't time," she said softly, her voice filled with a quiet resolve. "The corrupted magic—it's too strong. If I don't purify it, it will destroy the forest. And I can't let that happen."

Fenn tightened his grip on her hand, his eyes glistening with unshed tears. "Lira, please," he pleaded, his voice breaking. "There has to be another way. You can't—"

"I have to," Lira interrupted gently. She reached up with her free hand, cupping his face, her touch trembling. "Fenn… you've been my friend, my ally, and so much more. But this is my path."

Fenn shook his head, a tear slipping down his cheek. "You don't have to do this alone," he whispered, his voice choked with grief.

Lira felt her own tears welling up, but she pushed them down, focusing on the warmth of his touch, the feeling of being grounded in the moment. She held onto that sensation, even as she felt the Song pulling her further away. "I'm not alone," she replied, her voice steady despite the storm inside her. "I have you. And I have the spirits. And that's enough."

The ground beneath them trembled, the walls of the Nexus groaning as the city continued to collapse. Lira could feel the corrupted energy still lingering in the air, a dark, suffocating presence that threatened to swallow everything if she let it. She took a deep breath, feeling the Song's power building within her, the ancient melody urging her towards a final choice.

"Lira, don't," Fenn whispered, his voice barely audible.

Lira leaned forward, pressing her forehead against his, her voice barely more than a breath. "Thank you, Fenn," she murmured. "For everything."

Before Fenn could respond, she pulled away, her heart breaking at the look of anguish on his face. She turned to face the center of the Nexus, where the corrupted energy still pulsed like a dark wound in the air. The Song was stronger now, its notes weaving through her thoughts, pulling her towards the inevitable.

"Spirits of Elaria," Lira whispered, her voice filled with both hope and sorrow. "If you can hear me... lend me your strength."

The spirits responded with a quiet murmur, their presence like a warm breeze against her skin. She could feel their trust, their gratitude, and their sorrow mingling with her own. They knew what she was about to do, and they were ready to stand with her until the end.

Lira raised her hand, calling upon the Song's final verse. The melody shifted, its notes turning from a quiet hum to a powerful crescendo, resonating with the very roots of the earth. She could feel the ancient magic flowing through her, a connection that was both beautiful and terrible. It was a force that demanded everything from her, a sacrifice that would sever her bond with Elaria forever.

The corrupted energy writhed and twisted, fighting against the purifying power of the Song. Lira could feel the darkness pushing back, threatening to consume her, but she held on, focusing on the spirits' whispers and the memory of the forest she loved.

"Let this be my final gift," she whispered, her voice trembling. "To Elaria, and to all who call it home."

The energy around her surged, and for a moment, Lira felt as if she were standing at the edge of an abyss, the darkness pulling at her, threatening to drag her under. But then she heard the spirits' voices, their whispers like a chorus of hope, and she knew she couldn't give in.

She let go.

The Song's final note rang out, a pure, resonant sound that cut through the darkness like a blade of light. The corrupted energy shuddered, its dark tendrils dissolving into mist as the purifying magic washed over it. Lira felt the connection between herself and the forest snap, a sharp, searing pain that left her gasping for breath.

The world around her seemed to blur, the edges of reality fading as the Song's power faded into silence. Lira closed her eyes, a single tear slipping down her cheek, and for a moment, she felt a sense of peace—a quiet certainty that she had done what was right.

As the darkness closed in, she heard Fenn's voice, distant and filled with grief. "Lira!" he cried, his voice breaking with desperation.

But Lira couldn't respond. The Song had taken everything from her, and all she could do was let it go.

For Elaria.

Chapter 14
Rallying the Spirits

Lira stepped into the grove, the air heavy with a suffocating stillness. The leaves, usually rustling with the gentle murmur of the spirits' voices, hung motionless. The whispers she had grown so accustomed to were faint, barely audible, like echoes fading into the distance. It felt as though the very breath of Elaria was holding back, unsure whether to welcome her or turn away.

She reached the center of the grove, her heart pounding as she called out, "Elder Sylla?"

For a long moment, there was no response. Lira felt a chill run down her spine, the emptiness around her deepening the sense of isolation gnawing at her heart.

"Elder Sylla?" she called again, more urgently this time.

A sigh, like the sound of wind rustling through dry leaves, answered her. Slowly, the gnarled bark of the largest tree shifted, revealing Elder Sylla's weary face. The ancient spirit's eyes, once bright with the wisdom of ages, were dull, shadowed with a weariness that went beyond physical exhaustion.

"Lira," Sylla murmured, her voice carrying none of the warmth it once had. "You have returned."

"I…" Lira swallowed hard, fighting the urge to run. "I came to—"

"Why have you returned?" another voice interrupted, harsh and accusing. A younger spirit emerged from the shadows, her eyes sharp with anger. "To tell us of more failed alliances? To remind us that Ironhold's threat grows stronger while we stand powerless?"

Lira flinched at the words, her breath catching in her throat. "No, I—"

"What else can you offer us, Guardian?" the younger spirit continued, her tone cutting through Lira's defenses like a blade. "We put our trust in you, and now the forest suffers. The Breath of Elaria grows weaker with each passing day."

"Please," Lira pleaded, her voice shaking. "I know I failed to secure the Fae's support, but I'm trying to—"

"To what?" the younger spirit demanded, her voice rising. "To save us? To protect the forest? You are only one mortal, Lira, and the weight of this burden is too great for you alone."

The words struck Lira like a physical blow, and she felt the familiar weight of doubt pressing down on her, heavy and suffocating. She looked to Elder Sylla, hoping for some sign of support, but the ancient spirit only sighed, her eyes closing as if in defeat.

"Lira," Sylla murmured, her voice barely more than a whisper. "The spirits are afraid. They are losing faith—not only in you, but in the very hope of salvation. The Breath of Elaria falters, and with it, so does our strength."

"I know," Lira replied, her voice barely holding together. "But I'm doing everything I can to—"

"Everything?" the younger spirit scoffed, bitterness dripping from her words. "You have done nothing but stumble in the darkness, chasing alliances that were never meant to be."

"I'm trying to find a way," Lira insisted, her voice growing desperate. "I'm trying to—"

"Trying is not enough!" the younger spirit snapped, her eyes blazing with anger. "We need action! We need a leader who can protect us, not empty promises and broken words."

Lira felt her resolve crumbling, her hands trembling as she tried to keep her composure. She turned to the other spirits, searching their faces for any hint of support, but all she saw were expressions of doubt and despair.

"Please," Lira whispered, her voice breaking. "I just need more time."

"Time is a luxury we no longer have," Elder Sylla replied softly, her voice laced with sorrow. "The forest's strength wanes, and with each passing day, the shadows of Ironhold creep closer."

"But I…" Lira's voice faltered, her words catching in her throat. She could feel the connection to the forest slipping away, like sand slipping through her fingers. "I don't know what else to do."

The younger spirit's eyes softened slightly, but her voice remained firm. "You are not alone in this struggle, Lira," she said quietly. "But if you cannot find the strength within yourself, how can we find the strength to follow you?"

Lira felt a tear slip down her cheek, her shoulders slumping under the weight of her failures. She had tried so hard to be the guardian the forest needed, but all she had done was fail, time and time again. And now, the spirits were paying the price for her mistakes.

"I'm sorry," Lira whispered, her voice barely audible. "I'm so sorry…"

"Words of regret will not mend what is broken," Elder Sylla murmured, her voice filled with a deep, ancient sadness. "But neither will despair."

Lira looked up, meeting the elder spirit's gaze, and saw a flicker of something—something fragile and fleeting, like a dying ember in the darkness.

"There is still hope," Elder Sylla continued, her voice barely more than a whisper. "But you must find the strength to ignite it, Lira. If you falter now, the Breath of Elaria may be lost forever."

"I don't…" Lira began, her voice trembling. "I don't know if I can."

"Then you must decide," Elder Sylla replied softly, "whether you are truly the guardian the forest chose, or if you are merely a mortal child lost in the woods."

The words struck Lira to her core, and she felt the weight of her choices pressing down on her like a storm cloud. She wanted to argue, to insist that she was more than just a frightened girl stumbling in the dark. But all she could feel was the emptiness where her connection to the forest had once been—a hollow void that threatened to swallow her whole.

"I need to think," Lira murmured, her voice barely holding together. "I need… I need some time."

Elder Sylla's branches creaked softly as she inclined her head. "Then go," she said quietly. "But remember, Lira—time is running out."

Lira turned and stumbled away from the grove, the voices of the spirits fading behind her. She could still hear the faint echoes of their fear and doubt, each whisper cutting into her like shards of glass. She didn't know where she was going, only that she needed to be anywhere but here—away from the weight of their expectations, their disappointment.

As she walked, the forest seemed to close in around her, the trees looming like silent sentinels. The path ahead was uncertain, and Lira could feel her resolve slipping, the doubt gnawing at her like a relentless tide.

She had tried so hard to be the guardian the forest needed. But now, standing at the edge of despair, she couldn't help but wonder if she had been wrong all along.

The Chancellor's office was a stark contrast to the rest of Ironhold's imposing headquarters. While the factory floors below were filled with the relentless clang of machinery and the murmur of engineers discussing schematics, the Chancellor's space was silent and pristine. The walls were adorned with maps of Elaria and blueprints of the latest spirit engine models, laid out with meticulous precision. In the center of the room, a large oak desk stood, and behind it, Chancellor Corvin was reviewing reports with an air of composed intensity.

"Reports indicate resistance at multiple points within the forest," one of the advisors stated, her voice steady but tinged with unease. She held a set of rolled parchments, the edges marked with the seal of Ironhold's intelligence division. "Our scouts have confirmed sightings of the girl, Lira, among the spirit groves. She's stirring the spirits, gaining their loyalty."

The Chancellor didn't look up, his fingers drumming thoughtfully on the arm of his chair. "The forest's loyalty won't matter if we can render their resistance irrelevant," he said, his voice as cold and calculated as the room itself. "What about the extraction rates?"

"Steadily increasing, sir," the advisor replied. "But we've had… minor disruptions. The new engines are performing well under pressure, but there have been instances of resistance from the spirits, pushing back harder than anticipated."

"Harder than anticipated," the Chancellor repeated, his tone contemplative. "The girl's influence is growing, then. She's disrupting the natural order. This is unacceptable."

Another advisor, standing near the large map of Elaria, cleared his throat. "Chancellor Corvin, there's a concern that pushing extraction at this pace could—"

"The pace," Corvin interrupted, his voice barely more than a whisper yet commanding all the same, "is precisely what it needs to be. The expansion into the forest cannot slow, not now."

"But sir," the advisor continued cautiously, "the increased extraction rates are putting strain on the engines. Fenn has expressed concerns about—"

"Fenn is an engineer, not a strategist," Corvin cut in sharply, turning his piercing gaze on the advisor. "He will do what is necessary to ensure the engines remain operational. We cannot afford distractions from those who lack vision."

The room fell silent, the air thick with unspoken tension. Corvin's fingers stilled, and he leaned back in his chair, his eyes narrowing as he stared at the maps before him. After a moment, he let out a slow breath, a thin smile spreading across his lips.

"Lira may have the forest's loyalty, but loyalty without power is meaningless," he murmured, more to himself than to the advisors. "We will press forward with the next phase. Double the containment parameters and instruct the engineers to deploy the more advanced models. If resistance grows, we will crush it."

"Yes, sir," the advisors echoed in unison, a mixture of fear and resolve in their voices.

Meanwhile, in the heart of Ironhold's engineering sector, Fenn stood amidst a row of engines, their containment runes glowing faintly in the dim light. He adjusted his glasses, trying to focus on the adjustments laid out in front of him, but his mind was elsewhere. Ever since his encounter with Lira and the revelation of what the engines were truly doing, Fenn had been plagued by doubt. The cries of the spirits, once easy to dismiss, now felt like a constant presence, gnawing at his conscience.

"Fenn!" Brayden's voice pulled him from his thoughts. He turned to see his colleague approaching, his face set in a grim expression. "We've got new orders from the Chancellor. He wants the advanced models prepared for deployment by the end of the week."

"End of the week?" Fenn repeated, trying to mask his unease. "That's... sooner than planned."

"Yeah, well, the Chancellor's in a hurry," Brayden replied with a shrug. "Something about increased resistance in the forest. He wants to tighten the containment protocols and boost extraction efficiency."

Fenn felt a knot tighten in his stomach. "What does that mean for the engines?" he asked cautiously.

"It means we're going to be doubling the containment runes," Brayden explained, his voice carrying an edge of frustration. "And it means pushing the spirits harder to get the same amount of energy."

Fenn swallowed hard, feeling the weight of the words settle over him like a heavy fog. He knew what that meant—more strain on the spirits, more pain, and more chances for something to go wrong.

"Is this really necessary?" he asked quietly, glancing around to make sure no one else was listening. "We're already pushing the limits—if we keep escalating—"

"You sound just like you did last time," Brayden cut in, his voice low but firm. "This is what we signed up for, Fenn. The Chancellor knows what he's doing."

"Does he?" Fenn muttered, more to himself than to Brayden. "Or does he just know what he *wants*?"

Brayden sighed, rubbing the back of his neck. "Look, I don't like this any more than you do," he admitted. "But if we start questioning orders now, we're putting everything at risk. The expansion, the progress we've made—it all hinges on us doing our part."

Fenn didn't respond, his mind racing. He could still hear Lira's voice in his memory, filled with a desperate determination to protect the forest. He could feel the lingering echoes of the spirits' pain, growing louder with each passing day.

"Fenn," Brayden said, his tone more insistent. "Are you with me on this?"

Fenn looked at his friend, seeing the fear and uncertainty lurking behind his eyes. It was the same fear that had driven so many of them to follow orders without question, the same fear that kept them all complicit in something terrible.

"I'm with you," Fenn lied, his voice steady despite the turmoil inside.

Brayden nodded, relief flooding his face. "Good. We'll get through this."

As Brayden walked away, Fenn turned back to the engines, staring at the runes that glowed with an eerie, unsettling light. He knew that the time for hesitation was running out. If he didn't act soon, the damage would become irreversible—not just to the spirits, but to everything Lira and the forest stood for.

And the longer he stayed silent, the more he felt like he was betraying something far more important than orders or progress. He was betraying the very essence of what it meant to be human.

The grove was darker than Lira remembered, the once vibrant leaves now tinged with a grayish pallor, as if reflecting the spirits' despondency. The air felt thick with unspoken fears, and Lira could feel the weight of their doubt pressing down on her like a heavy storm cloud. But she refused to let the fear take hold of her. Not this time.

She stood at the center of the grove, facing the scattered spirits that had gathered reluctantly at her call. Elder Sylla and several of the younger spirits watched her with wary eyes, their expressions unreadable. Lira could feel their hesitation, their mistrust, but she pushed down her own doubts and spoke, her voice steady despite the storm brewing within her.

"Thank you all for coming," Lira began, her voice clear and resonant. "I know you're tired of words, tired of empty promises. I know I've failed you—more than once."

There was a murmur among the spirits, a low, rippling sound like the rustling of dry leaves. Lira took a deep breath and continued.

"I won't make excuses for my failures," she said firmly. "I came to you with hopes of alliances that never came to pass. I tried to secure support from the Fae, and they turned me away. I tried to stop Ironhold's expansion, and still they push further into the heart of Elaria."

Lira paused, searching their faces for any sign of understanding. Some spirits met her gaze, but others looked away, their eyes filled with doubt and resignation. She felt her chest tighten, but she forced herself to speak.

"I've made mistakes," Lira admitted, her voice faltering slightly. "But I'm not here to ask for forgiveness or to pretend that I can fix this on my own. I'm here because I refuse to give up on Elaria, and I refuse to let the Breath of Elaria fade into nothing."

"Why should we trust you now?" a voice interrupted—one of the younger spirits, his eyes narrowed with suspicion. "What makes this time different from all the others?"

Lira turned to face the spirit, meeting his gaze with unwavering determination. "Because this time," she said softly, "I'm not asking you to follow me blindly. I'm asking you to listen, and to choose what you believe in—whether it's me or the future of this forest."

The younger spirit hesitated, his expression softening slightly, but he remained silent. Lira took a step forward, raising her voice so that all could hear.

"I have journeyed through the heart of Elaria, from the outer groves to the ancient paths," she continued, her voice gaining strength. "I've spoken with the oldest spirits, faced the shadows of Ironhold, and felt the pain of this forest in my very soul. And I know that if we do nothing—if we let fear and doubt control us—Ironhold will destroy everything we hold dear."

"Empty words," another spirit murmured, but the bitterness in her voice lacked conviction.

"Maybe they are just words," Lira replied, her tone defiant. "But words are all I have left to offer you. I'm not a spirit. I don't have the ancient wisdom of Elder Ashen or the power of the Breath. All I have is my resolve, and my willingness to fight, no matter the cost."

There was a heavy silence, and Lira felt her heart pounding in her chest. This was it—the moment that would decide whether the spirits still had any faith left in her. She took a deep breath and lowered her voice, speaking from the heart.

"I'm not asking you to trust me because I'm perfect or because I have all the answers," she said softly. "I'm asking you to trust that I believe in this forest, in you, and in the strength we have when we stand together."

The murmur of doubt grew quieter, replaced by a hushed anticipation. Lira could feel their eyes on her, waiting for something more—something real.

"And if you can't trust me," Lira continued, her voice shaking slightly, "then trust in the land you've protected for centuries. Trust in the spirits that came before us, in the Breath of Elaria that still holds life within these roots. Trust in each other."

A low, creaking sound interrupted her, and Lira turned to see the largest tree in the grove shifting, its bark parting to reveal a weathered face. Elder Sylla emerged slowly, her eyes heavy with age and burden, but there was a glimmer of something in her gaze—something Lira had not seen in her before.

"Your words are bold, Lira of Elaria," Elder Sylla said, her voice like a whisper carried by the wind. "But words alone cannot bind what has been broken."

"I know," Lira replied, bowing her head. "That's why I'm not asking for words. I'm asking for your strength."

Elder Sylla's branches swayed slightly, and the other spirits turned to her, waiting for her response. The ancient spirit was silent for a long moment, her eyes closed as if listening to the whispers of the forest itself. When she finally spoke, her voice was heavy with the weight of ages.

"You seek our strength," she murmured. "But the strength you ask for comes at a great price. The Breath of Elaria is not merely a source of power—it is the lifeblood of all who dwell within this forest. To draw upon it fully is to risk the very foundation of what binds us to this land."

Lira felt a shiver run down her spine, but she met the elder spirit's gaze steadily. "I understand," she said quietly. "But I'm willing to pay that price if it means saving Elaria."

Elder Sylla studied her for a long moment, her expression unreadable. The other spirits held their breath, the tension in the air palpable. Finally, the ancient spirit nodded, her branches creaking softly.

"Very well," Elder Sylla said, her voice like a sigh. "You have shown us your resolve, and we cannot ignore the truth of your words. If you are willing to bear the burden, we will lend you our strength."

There was a murmur of surprise among the younger spirits, but Lira felt a rush of emotion—gratitude, relief, and fear all mingling into one. She bowed her head deeply, her voice trembling as she spoke.

"Thank you," she whispered, her heart pounding in her chest.

Elder Sylla's branches reached out, brushing lightly against Lira's forehead. "But know this, child of the forest," she warned softly. "The path you walk is fraught with danger, and the cost of drawing upon our strength may be greater than you can bear."

"I'm ready," Lira replied, her voice firm despite the lingering fear in her heart. "Whatever the cost, I will pay it."

The ancient spirit nodded, her eyes heavy with sadness. "Then let it be so," she said quietly.

The other spirits began to gather around Lira, their whispers filling the air like a chorus of winds. Lira closed her eyes, feeling their presence envelop her, their strength flowing into her like the roots of a great tree reaching deep into the earth. It was overwhelming, and for a moment, she felt as if she might be swept away by the sheer force of it.

But then she steadied herself, her resolve hardening into something unbreakable. She would not falter—not now, not when the future of Elaria depended on her. She would face whatever came, and she would not face it alone.

For the first time in a long time, Lira felt a flicker of hope—small and fragile, but real. And she held onto it with all the strength she had left.

Chapter 15
The Breath of Elaria

Ironhold was not the same city it once was. The once towering walls of iron had crumbled in places, revealing patches of earth that had been untouched by sunlight for decades. The air, which had always held the metallic tang of smoke and steam, now carried the fresh scent of wildflowers and the distant hum of new life. Change was everywhere, both subtle and sweeping, but perhaps nowhere was it more evident than within the heart of the city—the place where the old and the new were slowly learning to coexist.

Fenn stood at the edge of a vast clearing where the Alchemical Nexus had once loomed. Now, in its place, were the beginnings of something new—a project that could redefine the future of Ironhold. Tall, slender trees were beginning to sprout where the iron pillars had once been. Fenn could feel the tension in the air, the uncertainty of the people around him, but he also felt the potential, the hope that came with each day of rebuilding.

He took a deep breath, the air clear and crisp in a way that felt almost unfamiliar. The wind carried the distant echoes of conversations, the sound of hammers striking metal, and the gentle rustle of leaves that had only just begun to grow. It was a new kind of song—a quieter, more harmonious melody than the relentless pounding of machinery that had once dominated this place.

"Fenn?" A voice called from behind him. It was Mara, her steps light and quick as she approached. Her expression was thoughtful, her eyes reflecting the uncertainty of their task. "The council is ready for you."

Fenn nodded, turning away from the clearing and the memories it held. He felt the weight of his new role, the expectations of those who had trusted him to lead the city into a new era. He wasn't sure he was ready for it, but there was no turning back now.

Mara fell into step beside him, her voice quieter now. "Are you nervous?" she asked, a faint smile tugging at her lips.

"A little," Fenn admitted, though 'a little' was an understatement. He was terrified, but he couldn't let that show. "It's a lot of responsibility."

Mara glanced at him, a flicker of amusement in her eyes. "I never thought I'd see you as a politician," she said, her tone teasing. "Or a diplomat."

Fenn chuckled softly, shaking his head. "Neither did I," he replied. "But here we are."

They reached the newly constructed meeting hall, a modest building made of both iron and stone, its walls softened by vines and flowering plants. It was a symbol of the new path Ironhold was taking—one that integrated both the strength of its past and the harmony of nature. Fenn took a deep breath before pushing open the door and stepping inside.

The room was filled with the council members—engineers, Fae representatives, and even a few of the forest's Wild Ones who had taken on humanoid forms to communicate more easily with the humans. There was a tension in the air, a cautious curiosity as they all turned to face him. This was the first meeting of its kind, the first step towards something that had never been attempted before.

Fenn took a deep breath and faced them, his voice steady despite the nerves twisting in his gut. "Thank you all for coming," he began, his gaze sweeping the room. "I know that trust is… difficult after everything we've been through. But we have a chance to do something different—to rebuild Ironhold in a way that respects the balance of Elaria, rather than fighting against it."

One of the engineers, an older man named Garrick, crossed his arms and raised an eyebrow. "You want us to abandon everything we've built?" he asked, his voice carrying a hint of skepticism.

"Not abandon," Fenn replied, meeting Garrick's gaze evenly. "But adapt. What we've built here—our technology, our engineering—it doesn't have to be at odds with nature. The old ways of Ironhold were about domination, about controlling the world around us. But we don't have to do that anymore. We can use our knowledge to create something better."

There were murmurs of agreement from some of the council members, but others remained silent, their expressions uncertain. Fenn took another breath, his mind racing. He had spent days preparing for this moment, going over every word, every argument, but now that he was here, he found himself speaking from the heart.

"Lira showed me that the forest isn't just a resource to be harvested," he continued, his voice growing stronger. "It's a living thing, and it has its own wisdom, its own magic. If we can find a way to integrate that magic with our technology, we can build a city that's stronger and more sustainable than anything Ironhold has ever been."

One of the Fae representatives, a woman named Elowen with silver hair and eyes like moonlight, tilted her head thoughtfully. "You speak of balance," she said, her voice soft but clear. "But balance is not easily achieved. It requires trust, patience, and the willingness to listen."

Fenn nodded, feeling the truth of her words. "I know," he replied. "And I don't expect this to be easy. But I believe it's worth trying."

Elowen studied him for a moment before inclining her head. "Then we will listen," she said quietly. "And we will see what this new path holds."

Garrick let out a heavy sigh, running a hand through his greying hair. "You're asking for a lot, Fenn," he muttered. "But... I suppose if anyone can pull this off, it's you."

Fenn felt a flicker of relief, but he didn't let it show. Instead, he offered a small, grateful nod. "Thank you," he said sincerely. "For giving this a chance."

As the meeting continued, Fenn could feel the tension in the room slowly easing, replaced by a cautious optimism. It wasn't much, but it was a start—a fragile, tentative first step towards something new. He knew that there would be challenges ahead, that the path to a true balance between Ironhold and Elaria would be long and difficult. But he also knew that they weren't walking it alone.

When the meeting finally ended, and the council members began to disperse, Mara approached Fenn with a wry smile. "You didn't do half bad," she said, her tone teasing. "For a diplomat."

Fenn chuckled, the tension in his chest finally beginning to loosen. "Thanks," he replied, his voice light. "But this is just the beginning."

Mara's smile softened, and she placed a hand on his shoulder. "You're doing the right thing, Fenn," she said quietly. "And I think Lira would be proud."

Fenn felt a lump form in his throat, but he swallowed it down, nodding in silent acknowledgment. He couldn't bring back what had been lost, but he could honor it by building something new—something that Lira had always believed in.

A new balance was possible, and Fenn was determined to see it through. One step at a time.

The forest had changed, and yet it felt the same. Sunlight filtered through the canopy, casting patterns of light and shadow on the forest floor. Birds called to one another, and the breeze carried the scent of moss and earth. It was a scene that Lira had known all her life, but now it felt distant, almost like a memory that didn't quite belong to her.

Lira stood at the edge of a small clearing, watching as new saplings grew among the remnants of old, charred stumps. It was a symbol of what they had achieved—a new beginning rising from the ashes of the past. But despite the beauty around her, she felt a hollowness where the whispers of the spirits should have been.

A rustle in the underbrush drew her attention, and she turned to see Kara approaching. The Fae leader moved with the grace of someone who was both a part of the forest and above it, her steps light and purposeful. Her silver hair, once immaculate and regal, was now tousled by the breeze, and her expression was thoughtful as she approached Lira.

"Kara," Lira greeted her, her voice quieter than she intended. There were so many emotions tangled within her—anger, gratitude, grief, and hope—but she didn't know how to express them.

"Guardian," Kara replied, her voice as sharp as ever, but there was a softness in her tone that hadn't been there before. She stopped a few feet away from Lira, her eyes narrowing slightly as she studied her. "Or perhaps that title no longer applies."

Lira felt a pang of loss at Kara's words, but she managed a faint smile. "I suppose not," she said, her voice tinged with both regret and acceptance. "Not anymore."

Kara was silent for a moment, her gaze lingering on Lira as if she were trying to decipher a puzzle. "You gave up a great deal," she said quietly, her voice laced with something that almost sounded like respect. "More than I ever expected you would."

"I did what needed to be done," Lira replied, trying to keep her voice steady. She looked away, her gaze drifting to the saplings growing in the clearing. "It wasn't just for the spirits. It was for all of us."

Kara tilted her head, her eyes thoughtful. "Perhaps," she murmured. "But sacrifices are not easily made, nor are they easily forgotten."

Lira turned back to face her, searching for something in Kara's expression that would tell her if the Fae leader truly understood. "I didn't do it alone," she said softly. "You were there with me. You fought alongside me, even when we didn't trust each other."

Kara let out a quiet sigh, the sound almost lost in the rustling leaves. "Trust is not something I give lightly," she admitted. "And yet... you earned it, Guardian."

Lira blinked, taken aback by the admission. She had never expected to hear those words from Kara—never expected that the woman who had once viewed her with suspicion and disdain would offer her trust. It was a small thing, but in that moment, it felt like a gift.

"Thank you," Lira said, her voice barely more than a whisper.

Kara's gaze softened, and she inclined her head slightly. "We are all learning to trust," she replied. "It is a difficult thing to ask, especially after so much has been lost."

The two of them stood in silence for a moment, the weight of their shared experiences hanging heavy between them. The old grudges, the mistrust that had once defined their relationship—it was all fading in the face of what they had accomplished together.

Lira took a deep breath, gathering her courage. "Kara," she began, her voice hesitant. "I know we haven't always seen eye to eye. And I know I've made mistakes—mistakes that cost lives."

Kara raised an eyebrow, her expression unreadable. "You did what you thought was right," she said. "And I did what I believed was necessary to protect the forest. We both made choices that we cannot change."

"I know," Lira replied, her voice barely more than a breath. "But I want to find a way forward. For the spirits, for the forest... and for Ironhold."

Kara was silent for a long moment, her eyes narrowing as if weighing Lira's words. Finally, she spoke, her voice carrying the weight of a decision that had taken years to reach. "I once believed that humans and the forest were destined to be at odds," she said quietly. "But you have shown me that perhaps… there is another way."

Lira felt a flicker of hope, and she took a step closer, her voice trembling with the weight of her plea. "If we work together," she said, "we can build something new—something that honors the spirits and the people."

Kara let out a quiet sigh, and for a moment, Lira thought she might refuse. But then the Fae leader inclined her head, a faint, reluctant smile tugging at the corners of her lips. "You are stubborn, Guardian," she said, her tone almost teasing. "But perhaps that is not such a terrible quality."

Lira couldn't help but smile, the weight of her fear easing slightly. "Is that a yes?" she asked, her voice tinged with cautious optimism.

Kara's smile faded, replaced by a look of quiet determination. "It is a beginning," she replied. "Nothing more."

"A beginning is all we need," Lira said softly, her voice filled with gratitude.

Kara inclined her head once more, and for a moment, the two of them simply stood there, sharing a quiet understanding that had once seemed impossible. They were not friends, not yet, but they were something else—something stronger. Allies, perhaps, or partners in rebuilding a world that had been shattered.

Kara turned to leave, but before she did, she glanced back at Lira, her eyes reflecting a mixture of sadness and resolve. "Your sacrifice will not be forgotten," she said quietly. "And I will honor it by working towards a future where such sacrifices are no longer necessary."

Lira watched her go, her heart heavy with both loss and hope. She knew that the path ahead would be difficult, that there were still old wounds that needed to heal and old grudges that needed to be set aside. But for the first time in a long time, she felt a sense of peace—however fragile—that they were on the right path.

And in the quiet aftermath of everything they had endured, that was enough.

The forest felt different to Lira now. The air, once so alive with the whispers of spirits and the steady rhythm of Elaria's ancient heartbeat, was silent. It was a silence that pressed in on her, not oppressive but poignant, as if the trees were holding their breath. She walked along the familiar path leading to the edge of the forest, her steps slow and deliberate, taking in the sights that had been her home and her charge for so long.

The sunlight filtered through the leaves, casting dappled patterns on the ground. Birds flitted between branches, their songs light and carefree. To anyone else, it would seem that the forest was unchanged, as eternal and steadfast as the roots beneath her feet. But to Lira, it felt like a place that had become foreign, as if she were a visitor in a home that no longer belonged to her.

She paused by a large oak tree, its bark rough and weathered with age. Her fingers brushed against the familiar grooves, but there was no answering pulse, no gentle recognition from the spirit within. The absence was like a physical ache, a reminder of what she had severed to protect Elaria.

"You don't have to leave," a voice broke through the silence. It was Fenn, his voice soft but steady. He stood a few steps behind her, watching her with an expression she couldn't quite read. Concern, perhaps, or maybe it was sadness.

Lira didn't turn to face him. "I can't stay," she replied, her voice barely more than a whisper. "I don't belong here anymore."

Fenn took a hesitant step closer, his eyes searching hers. "You could help rebuild," he said. "There's still so much to be done. Ironhold is changing, the forest is healing... We need you, Lira."

She shook her head, the weight of her decision heavy in her chest. "No, Fenn," she said, her voice tinged with regret. "The Guardian of Elaria is gone. The bond I had with the forest... it's gone, too."

Fenn's shoulders slumped slightly, his hands clenched at his sides as if searching for something to hold onto. "I wish there was a way to make this right," he murmured, his voice thick with emotion. "To give you back what you lost."

Lira finally turned to face him, offering a small, sad smile. "What I lost isn't something that can be given back," she said gently. "It was a part of me, and now it's not. And that's something I have to learn to live with."

There was a long, heavy silence between them, the weight of unspoken words hanging in the air. Fenn wanted to argue, to find a way to keep her here, but he could see the resolve in her eyes—the quiet certainty of someone who had already made peace with her choice, even if that peace was fragile.

"Where will you go?" he asked, his voice barely more than a whisper.

Lira looked away, her gaze drifting towards the distant horizon where the forest met the sky. "I don't know," she admitted. "But there's a world out there—a world that needs people to protect it. Maybe... maybe I can find a place in it."

Fenn took a step closer, his expression pained. "Lira, you—"

"Fenn," she interrupted softly, meeting his gaze. "You're doing exactly what you need to do. You're helping to rebuild, to create something better. You're leading them towards a future where humans and spirits can coexist. And that's exactly what Elaria needs."

"But what about what you need?" Fenn asked, his voice filled with frustration and sadness.

Lira took a deep breath, her gaze steady. "I need to find that on my own," she said quietly. "I need to find a way to move forward—to figure out who I am without the forest."

Fenn was silent, the fight leaving his shoulders. He understood, even if he didn't want to. "If you ever need a place to come back to," he said, his voice thick with emotion, "you'll always have one here. Always."

"Thank you," Lira replied, her voice soft. She reached out and squeezed his hand, a brief but meaningful gesture. It wasn't a goodbye—it was a promise, a connection that would remain, even if it was different now.

She turned and continued walking down the path, her footsteps carrying her away from the heart of Elaria. As she reached the edge of the forest, she paused, taking one last look at the place she had given everything to protect. The sunlight filtering through the trees seemed brighter, and the leaves rustled gently in the breeze, as if offering her a quiet farewell.

And then, just as she was about to step beyond the forest's edge, she heard it—a faint whisper, so soft that she almost thought she had imagined it. But it was there, a gentle murmur carried on the wind, like the distant echo of a memory.

"Thank you."

Lira closed her eyes, a tear slipping down her cheek. It wasn't the bond she had lost—it wasn't the deep connection to the spirits that had once been a part of her soul. But it was a reminder that the forest hadn't forgotten her, that her sacrifice had not gone unnoticed.

She took a deep breath and stepped beyond the edge of the forest, the path ahead of her stretching into the unknown. She didn't know where she was going or what she would find, but she knew she couldn't stay in the place that had once been her home. It was time to find a new path, to discover who she was now that everything had changed.

The wind picked up, carrying with it the scent of earth and leaves, and Lira walked forward, her heart heavy with loss but open to the possibilities of what lay ahead.

Elaria was no longer her world, but she had saved it. And now, she would find her place in the world she had given so much to protect.

Epilogue
A New Dawn

The forest of Elaria was silent, as if holding its breath in the aftermath of the final confrontation. The sky above, once clear and expansive, now carried the scars of the battle—a mixture of deep blues and violet streaks, hinting at the lingering presence of the magic that had been unleashed. The once relentless hum of Ironhold's machines had finally ceased, and in the quiet that followed, the forest seemed to sigh, a release of tension built up over ages of conflict and doubt.

Lira stood at the heart of the grove, her hand resting against the rough bark of Elder Ashen. She could still feel the pulse of Elaria beneath her fingers, though it was faint, like a heartbeat struggling to find its rhythm. The battle had taken a toll not just on the land, but on its spirits and its people. She closed her eyes, feeling the whispers of the trees around her, each one a gentle murmur of gratitude and mourning for those lost.

She had paid a heavy price to bring Ironhold's reign to an end. The Breath of Elaria had been restored, but not without cost— Lira could feel the lingering echoes of the pact she had made with the ancient spirits. Their power flowed through her now, strengthening the roots of the forest, binding her to its fate in a way that went beyond duty or birthright. She was no longer just the guardian of Elaria; she was a part of it, and it was a part of her.

"Lira?" a voice called softly from behind her.

She turned to see Fenn approaching, his face drawn and weary, but his eyes carrying a flicker of hope. His once-pristine engineer's uniform was now tattered, stained with mud and blood from the battle. Fenn had chosen his side, defying Ironhold and risking everything to stand with Lira and the spirits. It had been a journey fraught with uncertainty and inner turmoil, but he had made his choice in the end.

"The spirits…" he began, his voice thick with emotion. "Are they—?"

"They're healing," Lira replied, offering a faint smile. "It will take time, but the damage is not beyond repair."

Fenn let out a breath he hadn't realized he was holding, his shoulders slumping with relief. "I was afraid," he admitted quietly, "that after everything, we wouldn't be able to fix what we'd done."

Lira's smile faded slightly, and she turned her gaze back to the grove. "There are some things that can never be fully mended," she murmured. "But the forest endures, and so do we."

A gentle breeze swept through the clearing, carrying with it the scent of fresh earth and blooming wildflowers. It was a sign of renewal, a promise that Elaria's wounds would heal in time. Lira felt the weight of her own doubts and fears lift, carried away on the wind like leaves in autumn.

"Have you heard from the others?" Lira asked, her voice quieter now.

Fenn nodded. "The surviving engineers have agreed to dismantle what's left of the containment engines. They… they're starting to understand what we were really doing. It'll take time, but Ironhold is changing."

"It's a start," Lira replied, her tone hopeful. "And what about the Chancellor?"

Fenn's expression darkened momentarily, and he shook his head. "He's gone. The final surge of energy from the engines—when the pact broke—destroyed everything he had built. It's over."

Lira nodded slowly, absorbing the news. Corvin had been relentless in his pursuit of power, driven by a belief that Ironhold's ambitions were justified. His fall marked the end of an era—one defined by conquest and greed at the expense of balance. But the end of one era was the beginning of another, and it was up to those who remained to shape it.

As the breeze continued to rustle through the trees, a faint shimmer appeared in the air beside Lira, and a familiar voice spoke softly.

"You have done well, child of the forest," Elder Ashen's voice whispered, though the ancient spirit was no longer bound to a single tree. His presence was everywhere now, a part of the Breath of Elaria itself.

"Elder," Lira whispered, her voice barely audible. "Is it… truly over?"

"Not over," Elder Ashen replied, his tone both gentle and firm. "But this chapter has ended, and a new one begins. The forest will thrive once more, and you will guide it as its guardian."

Lira closed her eyes, feeling the connection between herself and the land strengthen with each passing moment. It was a daunting responsibility, but one she had accepted willingly. She opened her eyes and met Fenn's gaze, seeing the same determination reflected there.

"What will you do now?" she asked him softly.

Fenn hesitated, a wistful look crossing his face. "I don't know," he admitted. "Ironhold needs rebuilding, and there's so much to set right... But I think my place is here, helping you and the spirits."

Lira nodded, feeling a swell of gratitude for the friend she had found in the most unlikely of places. "Then we rebuild—together."

Days turned into weeks, and weeks into months. Under Lira's guidance, the spirits began to reclaim the land that had been scarred by Ironhold's ambitions. The younger spirits who had once been lost in despair found hope in Lira's unwavering resolve. With Fenn's help, the surviving engineers and villagers of Ironhold learned to respect the forest's boundaries and work alongside it rather than against it. It wasn't easy, and there were many who still clung to the old ways, but progress was being made.

The Fae, once distant and distrustful, began to cautiously re-enter the affairs of the forest. Lady Kara remained wary of Lira's intentions, but she could not deny the human's efforts to restore the balance. Over time, an unspoken truce formed between the Fae and the guardians of Elaria—a fragile alliance built on mutual respect and a shared desire to protect their home.

One day, as Lira walked the ancient paths of the forest, she felt a familiar presence beside her. Farael, the spirit creature who had watched over her since the beginning, emerged from the shadows, his eyes gleaming with quiet pride.

"You have come far, Guardian," Farael murmured, his voice like the rustle of autumn leaves.

"And yet there is still so much to do," Lira replied, her tone both weary and determined.

"That is the way of the forest," Farael said softly. "It is never truly still, never fully at rest. There will always be new challenges, new threats. But you have shown that you are strong enough to face them."

Lira smiled faintly, resting her hand on the spirit's head. "I couldn't have done it without you, Farael."

"Perhaps," Farael replied, his voice tinged with amusement. "But this path was yours to walk. You chose it, and you saw it through to the end."

Lira's smile widened slightly, and she let out a quiet sigh of contentment. For the first time in what felt like a lifetime, she felt a sense of peace—a sense that the future, though uncertain, was filled with promise.

As the sun dipped below the horizon, casting long shadows through the trees, Lira looked out over the forest she had fought so hard to protect. The wind carried with it the soft whispers of the spirits, their voices no longer filled with pain or fear, but with gratitude and hope.

Elaria was healing. The Breath of Elaria was strong once more, and the bonds that had been broken were beginning to mend.

And as long as Lira drew breath, she would ensure that Elaria's story continued—one chapter at a time.